Mixed Signals

A Collection of Short Stories

BETTY GRAHAM HOWARD

Copyright © 2011 by Betty Graham Howard. All rights reserved. No part of this book may be photocopied or otherwise reproduced without written permission from the author.

ISBN: 9781453859735
Printed in the United States of America

This collection of short stories is a work of fiction. The characters and situations bear no resemblance to reality and are purely figments of the author's imagination.

Contact the author: BGHOWARD@AOL.COM
Cover painting by Kay Beaubien
Layout and design by Sonya Unrein
Copyediting by Margie Arnold and Lois Hansen

Quote from *Walking Nature Home: A Life's Journey* by Susan J. Tweit. University of Texas Press, 2009. Used with permission by the author. All rights reserved.

To my precious daughter,
Anne,
who by her example
has led the way.

Contents

Marin County, California
Knitting At The Old Oak Table   11
The Alley   33
Buddies at the Bonfire   54
JJ Vineyards   74

Douglas County, Colorado
Use of Force   99
Pencil Pushin'   115

El Paso County, Colorado
Mixed Signals   136
Good Church People   149
Isabelle Weir   153

Custer County, Colorado
Amanda Harrington   176
Isabelle and Amanda   196

Epilogue
The Things She Knit   223

Acknowledgments

No book is created alone. I wish to thank those who have supported my efforts to write this collection of short stories. My editor, Margie Arnold, my editor-reader, Lois Hansen and my reader, Anne Hourigan, who each made astute suggestions. Every other Saturday for five years, the Kergyma Writing Group; John Konselman, Kay Scharff, Colette and Bob Sheets, Jerry Cox, Jo Anne Majors, and the late Marvin Beckman offered their insights. A writer needs the support of those who are knowledgeable as to writing expertise, and the Pikes Peak branch of the National League of American Pen Women with their professional standards served in this capacity. My brother Bob Graham and his wife, Nancy Graham, offered their economic support for which I am very grateful. Two friends, Elaine Kunzman offered me constant emotional support, and Dee Ring Martz, served as my ballast; neither have ever wavered in this support. Lastly my heartfelt gratitude goes to Sonya Unrein, who "rescued" this book. To all of the above, I am so very, very grateful.

"Stories nurture our connection to place and each other. They show us where we have been and where we go..."
—Susan J. Tweit, *Walking Nature Home: A Life's Journey*

Marin County, California

Knitting At The Old Oak Table
Sally's Story

Sally Boothe's knitting is drenched with tears. The yarn sits upon her lap, a soggy mess. No one seems alarmed by the soaked skeins of yarn except for me. I stare aghast at the sodden seven hundred and fifty dollars worth of designer wool. Sneaking a peek at the others to see how they are reacting, it appears everyone is determinedly concentrating upon their knitting, choosing to ignore what has just happened. The room is so still, the ticking of the old antique clock sounds as if it is booming. In communal silence with hunched shoulders and heads bowed over their needles, the group has chosen to direct its attention to their projects rather than to Sally's tears. Are they being heartless? I conclude they are probably considering Sally's breach of etiquette and are closing ranks in tribal unison to show their disapproval. Only Chancie's small gesture of quietly putting her fleshy arm around Sally's shoulders shows a hint of compassion.

For the past two hours, six of us have been sitting together at an old oak table in The Knitting Boutique. Rainbows of color march up and down the interior walls, which are overflowing with bins of designer yarns. Soft, lush alpacas; warm, sensible worsteds; glitzy silver, gold metallic, and thin gossamers of linen and silk have tempted us. With just one touch of the soft, sensual fibers, we are smitten. These enticements imported from far-away places such as Milan, Paris, Australia, the Aran and Shetland Isles and Russia have lured us into spending a fortune and signing up for a series of Fair Isle knitting lessons.

"Corrine, is this color too bold for Fair Isle?" asks tinsel-tressed Laura.

"Well, Fair Isle colors are pretty subdued," responds the proprietor.

"I remember hiking over the moors last July and the scenery was downright dull," mutters Chancie. "It was so foggy and misty you couldn't see a foot ahead of yourself. In fact there wasn't any color, it was all gray, if you call that a color."

As we make our yarn selections, most of the knitters are oblivious to the expense and appear to be making their choices with abandon. I feel a sense of envy. Having to constantly remind myself of cost, I choose yarn from a New England manufacturer, a sensible merino wool at a practical price. The others spend lavishly.

Those who have already made their decisions are engaged in intense conversation about the onset of "the season." The two tinseled blondes, Laura and Trisha, are explaining in elaborate detail their final fittings of their couture dresses for the upcoming gala opening of the 1974 San Francisco Opera. I secretly find it amusing no one seems to mention which opera is being performed.

Plump, matronly Chancie stoically announces to the group, "I'm going to have to wear my mother's antique olive lace shawl again over a basic black gown. God, I'm sick of it, and I'll bet you're all sick of seeing me in it."

A chorus of, "Oh no, no," ensues.

Chancie continues, "I can't even afford to buy a pair of Keds sneakers to wear out on the bay on our bucket, much less afford a new gown for the opera. Johnny continues to have all our money tied up in the stock market."

Oh my, here we go again with the usual litany of the few "old" rich, who sit at the table, complaining about being cash poor, as if it were a mantra. I find it highly amusing that in spite of them denigrating their seemingly threadbare existence, the group is absorbed in what is going to be very costly social entertaining. After the opening of the opera next Thursday evening, the season begins. There is a feverish pitch of elegant parties at the mansions on Belvedere Island, which overlook the San Francisco Bay.

In contrast to the old rich—the nouveau rich—Laura and Trisha, exquisitely attired in designer sweats with hair coiffed by the latest trendy hair dresser on Maiden Lane, are discussing the fittings of their gowns. Cost is no object. In fact their husbands demand they look as posh as possible no matter what the expense.

Laura complains about her fitter, "How dare he intimate I've gained ten pounds and my personal form will have to be re-done. I went in for my first fitting yesterday and he had the temerity to suggest I had gained weight. Now, obviously the dress was too tight. Was that my fault? But I have to put up with those innuendoes; he's the best dressmaker in town."

No one dares respond to Laura's comments. In unison our gazes quickly shift downward to our knitting as we sit around the oak table. There is enough room for all six of us to spread out our assorted Hebrides yarns without knocking elbows as we click away on our elegant, rosewood needles. Settling down we arrange our yarns by color in front of us. A few of the ladies are excessively engaged in praising each others' color choices. I've noticed over the course of our knitting sessions, there appears to be an incessant need to reassure and flatter. They have mastered the comforting social art of buoying each other up.

While I watch aghast as Brooksie paws through my yarns, "Super color selection, Penny, so refined. You have such a real sense of taste."

"Thank you Brooksie," I reply as I attempt to unobtrusively ease my yarns out of her reach. Her long blood-red fingernails are catching in my skeins. Why do overweight women pay so much attention to the adornment of their nails?

By the way, how's the job going?" she inquires.

"I love the work, Brooksie. It's really challenging and keeps my brain moving at top speed. But often the time pressures are unrelenting. It is so document intensive. I'm constantly at the computer re-doing wills and trusts." I grin at her. "Would you believe a state senator in Nevada, whom I shall not mention by name, asked me to use more complex words in his will. He said he was paying a fortune for these documents and he wanted the vocabulary to reflect that. He felt he didn't have to understand it. He even suggested I intersperse it with Latin to make it more scholarly."

Brooksie laughs with delight, "How hilarious!"

I continue on, "I haven't shared the senator's thoughts with Doug, who will review the will. As you can well imagine, after hearing all of this and realizing I have to deal with these types of clients, I'm glad I have my knitting to turn to for comfort when I arrive home in the evenings. It's so therapeutic."

She looks at me intently, "You know, I think I might have Stan call your attorney and set up an appointment for us. We sure need some advice about our assets and setting up an estate. We've been putting it off for years."

"That would be terrific Brooksie. My attorney, Doug Bauer, takes personal pride in adapting each estate planning document to his individual clients, so I know you won't be disappointed."

At this exact moment, I suddenly become aware; I am not truly a part of this group, not on their level, at least financially or socially. Was Brooksie considering me "the help" by offering to set up an appointment with the firm for which I worked? No, she was just being nice. But upon a few occasions in the past, I had become ill at ease in this company. I couldn't seem to bring myself to take part in some of their bantering conversation: the false flattery, the inexplicable complaining about not having enough money, the veiled remarks made by the old rich about the new. We share a common bond of a passion for knitting and I enjoy them immensely, but that's where the similarity in values seems to end.

I live west of Highway 101 in a three bedroom rancher tucked under the redwoods in the small village of Larkspur. My lifestyle bears no resemblance to that of my fellow knitters. Not having married into their tier of society and recently becoming a widow faced with raising a daughter by myself places me well below their social strata.

I occasionally envy the comfort of my fellow knitters. They appear to be so sheltered and protected from the hurly-burly of life. They reside east of Highway 101 in wealthy Belvedere and Tiburon. It's an East Egg/West Egg kind of thing, like Fitzgerald's *The Great Gatsby*. Gatsby stares yearningly across the inlet at the twinkling lights of Daisy Buchanan's huge mansion. Just like Gatsby standing on his dock looking across the inlet, I too yearn for what we both imagine to be the ultimate in lifestyles.

There is a shifting about at the table as we ready ourselves for the new complicated knitting stitch. Corrine Price, the eager overly-solicitous proprietor of the shop, is about to begin the lesson in the Continental. The women in Scotland traditionally utilize it, mastering it so well they are able to build up enormous speed and can produce an intricate sweater within a week. It encompasses picking at two skeins of different colored yarn and managing both at the same time, as you "pick" across a row. Corrine assures us mastering this stitch will be relatively easy, since she considers us all expert knitters.

After a great deal of hand-holding on her part and after an hour for each of us to make our color choices, we finally begin our lesson. The hand-holding is definitely worth it for Corrine, since each skein retails for fifty dollars and we have each purchased at least twelve skeins of yarn in order to complete our sweaters.

As we begin, she places Pachelbel's *Canon in D* in the tape deck knowing it will soothe the frayed nerves of this society-driven group. She advises us the calm temperate rhythm will aid our concentration. During these moments I've observed my knitting friends actually relax. Shoulders ease into their natural positions. Forced smiles disappear. Meeting the social demands of their upwardly mobile husbands is forgotten. They slouch over their yarns and kick off their finely tooled Farragamo flats. The pressure of having to reflect their husbands' status and look "just so" appears to vanish under the old oak table. They are able to set aside the demands of the constant car pooling of their teenagers up and down Highway 101; to the private school in San Rafael, to the tennis lessons at the Belvedere Tennis Club or over to Blacky's Pasture for a lacrosse game. This plethora of activities is meant to keep their teenagers infinitely busy and hopefully, off drugs and alcohol. These maternal responsibilities are now cast aside as they concentrate upon the mastery of the stitches.

After a half hour of silence, due to our concentration, we are interrupted by the phone. Corrine picks up and announces it's for blue-eyed, naturally blonde Sally Boothe, one of my favorites. Sally asks me to take the message, since I am closest to the phone and she is in the midst of a color change.

I listen carefully and after hearing the message, I falter, "It's Maria and she says Mr. Boothe has called to say he will be late coming down from Napa."

Sally shrugs.

I continue listening to Maria, but hesitate to relate it

in front of the group, "Sally, this message is quite personal. Don't you want to take it?"

Sally shakes her head, "No, you go on."

"Okay, Maria says Mr. Boothe wants you to be on your toes this evening. Dan Wood, his special client, will be in attendance. Remember to instruct the carver that Dan Wood likes his roast beef medium rare, sliced one-eighth of an inch thick. There is a lot riding on this twenty million dollar contract." I hesitate, taking a breath, "Sally, I'm not sure I should go on."

"Oh please, go ahead." She looks at the others. "You all might as well hear the bloody instructions Jim issues before a party."

"He said you're not to screw up this time. He doesn't want a repeat of past catastrophes such as the ice swan centerpiece filled with Beluga caviar melting all over the linen. Everything must be perfect."

All eyes are focused upon me wondering what's next. Those present have been blatantly eavesdropping, of course, although they pretend to be lost in their knitting. They are frowning. Sally's hands tremor slightly as she carefully shifts into a yarn change.

"Sally, I'm afraid I can't understand any more of Maria's excited chatter." I choose to hang up.

Chancie cuts in, "Oh, Sally don't give Jim any mind. My God, we all know snafus happen at these business soirees. Anything can go wrong. I remember when our caterer backed his truck into our kitchen for God's sake. Jim should loosen up."

Sally slowly shakes her head, "Well, Chancie, unfortunately Jim seems to be beyond that point. I find it difficult to deal with him anymore. We're going through a bad patch."

This revealing admission on Sally's part triggers an instant switch in conversation. No one wants to address what has just been shared. To ease the tension a heated discussion ensues about recipes for persimmon pudding. I almost laugh out loud, what a ludicrous topic after what we have just heard. But true to their form, they have chosen a safe subject to hide behind. The persimmons have reached a luscious glow this fall and something as mundane as pudding seems to be comforting. They banter about, attentively focusing on the pros and cons of the two alternatives for toppings. Is it going to be whipped cream or hard sauce? I have the temerity to suggest Cool-Whip. That remark is met with stunned silence and then giggles.

Chancie puts her needles down and stoutly asserts, "Hard sauce is the only topping for persimmon pudding. Johnny's mother, Mrs. Paige, always serves it that way and Grandmother Paige did too. When I douse a huge dollop of the cognac-laced hard sauce on the pudding, Johnny's eyes twinkle with affection for me. And believe you me, his eyes display that affection upon only too few occasions, I might add."

Tinsel-tressed Laura admonishes, "Oh, Chancie, it's too much to go to all of that trouble these days. Just whip up some heavy cream in the mixer."

"That's easy enough for you to say, Laura. What do you know about too much trouble? You have live-in help at your place. You can have them do whatever you want."

The phone rings again. Corrine picks up and announces it's Maria.

"I can't really understand her Sally, she sounds so agitated. I think she's saying the boys from the Tiburon Liquor Closet are making their delivery. Where should the wine and liquor be placed?"

"I don't know why Maria's becoming so unhinged, she knows the booze is always placed in the garage along the side wall next to my old Mercedes coupe." She determinedly focuses on another yarn change.

There is a nervous shifting at the table. Laura secretly rolls her eyes at Trish. Brooksie studies the passers-by as they stare into the window. Chancie repositions her pattern on the table. Brows furrow. I have a sense some of the participants want Sally to get her fanny down Tiburon Boulevard to her ivy covered home with its multiple views of the bay. They are well aware of what it takes to get a large catered affair *underway*.

Finally Chancie suggests just this, "Sally, don't you think you'd better pull yourself together and get out of here?"

"Oh, there's still time, Chancie. Maria knows all the ropes. She'll take care of the preparations. Besides, I'm just having too much fun with you darlings." She grins at all of us, "I don't want to go home and face the responsibilities of having to entertain for business. I hate it. When was the last time you and Johnnie were over for dinner, Chancie? It's been too long hasn't it? We don't even seem to make time to entertain our dearest friends any more."

"Listen Sally, we all hate entertaining for business! But what happens to business if we don't?"

Sally squiggles her nose and breaks into nervous laughter.

Brooksie quickly returns to the safe subject of persimmon pudding, "Chancie, do you ever give out your family recipe for persimmon pudding?"

"Of course not. I'd have to face the rancor of generations of Paige women rising out of their graves."

Finally, the corrugated ribbing on the colorful sweaters has been completed and with relief and satisfaction, we gush over each others' work. This would have been the appropriate time for Sally to leave, but with fixed determination she proceeds with the intricate Fair Isle pattern.

Corrine switches the cassette in the tape deck to the more soothing jazz of Szabo's guitar, sensing there is even more anxiety arising within the group. Heads are bent down in supposed concentration. The balmy late afternoon sun shines through the huge street-level windows and passers-by smile at what appear to be serene, relaxed upper middle-class women knitting away on their yarns.

The phone rings again. There is a collective hush. Corrine picks up.

"It's Maria," she shrugs. "She's asking which gown and what jewelry and shoes Miss Sally wants laid out."

Sally shakes her head, "Poor Maria, she's in a bind, tell her the gold Armani and the five-inch gold strapped heels. And all the heavy fourteen carat gold bangles in my jewelry box. The lady of the house must make a positive presentation of herself. After all, this is show biz!"

Now each knitter appears to be silently *willing* Sally on her way. They realize what's at stake. They are very close having served together for years on the Belvedere Club Board, and their focus on their teenagers' activities has resulted in their lives interweaving as firmly as the stitches they are knitting this fall afternoon. To some Sally's odd behavior has reached a point where it's downright alarming.

I finally break the silence. Now, I feel a need to ease the tension and following the behavior pattern of my fellow knitters, I, too, change the subject.

"Corrine, how about dinner at the Barbeque Pit after our lesson?"

"Sure, would anyone else like to join Penny and me?" she asks. Not including the others with an invitation would have been a breach of good manners in this set, although they had never joined us when invited in the past.

Sally comments, "How lucky you are to be able to eat barbeque. I haven't had decent ribs in years. I've always had to be pencil thin to fit into my clothes. Most of the time I'm starving to death."

I smile ruefully at her. The room is growing darker. The sun has eased its way over the Marin hills. It is almost time to leave. But unbelievably another call comes in; Corrine translates as best she can the loud, shrill agitated Spanish and English, which can be overheard by all.

"The caterer has arrived. Maria needs to know where he's supposed to place the bar, the steam tables and the ice statuary. And too, Mr. Boothe has called again en route and wants to know, where the hell his wife is?"

Sally remarks, "Aren't men terribly amusing? They've become so accustomed to knowing we will always be there, they simply go into shock when we aren't."

She suddenly rises, reaching for the phone. She speaks with deliberate care.

"Maria, please have the caterer set up next to the windows on the west wall as we usually do. It's always lovely for our guests to gaze at the sun setting beyond the Golden Gate Bridge. See that that view is left open and be sure the iced statuary is placed at the shaded end of the table under the redwoods."

She pauses and after taking a deep breath continues, "Now listen carefully, there's been a change. And because of this change, I'm going to give you a very large tip for this evening. You will have some additional duties. It might be a little more difficult for you, but you have always served our guests so beautifully and they all know and love you. I know I can depend upon you. You see, I won't be at the party. You'll have to manage it all by yourself."

The clicking of the elegant rosewood knitting needles abruptly comes to a halt.

Sally continues calmly, "If Mr. Boothe happens to call again, tell him I won't be attending the party, and rest assured I won't be screwing up again."

After hanging up the phone, Sally returns to her knitting and as I glance over at her to see if she is okay, I notice she is dropping some stitches. The cassette in the tape deck has finished. The room is absolutely still. She begins to weep quietly. Her tears flood down on her yarns. Brooksie sets her knitting aside and places her fleshy arm around Sally's taut shoulders.

"I'm sorry, I've got to have a cigarette," apologizes Chancie. Everyone understands Chancie's strong urge as she rummages through her threadbare purse for the antique jade cigarette holder.

All choose not to speak. Some with downcast eyes are buried in their own thoughts. Others appear to me to be silently considering the consequences of Sally's foolish actions. She continues her quiet weeping. Minutes pass and the weeping eventually subsides.

Suddenly the chime on the clock tower strikes five. As we all rise and shove our yarns into our carpetbags, which all bear similar colors and styles, none of us know quite what to do for or with Sally.

She does, however. She looks up at me and asks, "Could I join you and Corrine for barbeque and eat myself silly?"

I hug her.

We all grin at each other and sigh in communal relief. A few make a hasty retreat for the door as they murmur their good-byes.

"Call me, Sally," urges Chancie.

"Yes, me too," joins in Bootsie.

Upon hearing this, I suddenly wonder, will they call Sally?

* * * * *

After ribs at the Barbeque Pit, Sally and I drive over to my place. She's made another momentous decision. She's choosing not to return to her home this evening. What that portends we do not know. As the sun finally disappears in the west over the Marin hills and into the Pacific, we sit in the early evening light out on my deck sipping wine under the stately redwoods. We silently listen to the comforting sounds of the meandering creek. The playful rippling of the water appears to ease Sally's tension. Her facial features soften and her hunched shoulders lower to a more natural position. I choose not to engage her in conversation sensing she needs this quiet time to gather her thoughts.

Perhaps because of the wine or the need to unburden herself after the events of the day, she begins what is to be a revealing conversation, "I envy your autonomy, Penny. Your courage to make a go of it alone. I've felt trapped in this sorry state of a marriage for so long. You have no idea the toll it has taken." She grimaces, "The emptiness of entertaining people who aren't even friends. Knowing all of the business of socializing takes precedent over Jason and Jennifer's needs." She shakes her head, "I feel I should be the kids' champion, but I'm not strong enough to stand up against Jim. I don't understand what is happening to him. His personality has become so harsh and overbearing. Though, I know there's a lot of pressure on him."

She looks at me questioningly, expecting I guess, some kind of explanation on my part as to Jim's evolving behavior. I am unable to provide one.

"Sally, I don't think I can truly answer that. I don't know you all that well, least of all Jim. Our lives don't really intersect. From outward appearances, when I've seen you at lacrosse games, you've appeared to me to be the ideal family."

"That's an illusion. We are not happy. Every evening I set up dinner on the sideboard and retreat from the family on to the deck drinking some vintage wine and watching the sunset. And as I listen to Jim and the children, I become enraged with his way of dealing with them. His expectations of the kids almost borders on cruelty."

She pauses and furtively clutches at her hand-knit sweater, "I suppose I could handle it, if it were only me. When I take a good look, I realize the toll it is taking upon all of us. My rage overwhelms me. I'm exhausted because the anger takes up so much of my energy. It is so draining." She doesn't meet my eyes. "These past few months my behavior patterns are either napping or losing myself in wine. I have nothing left for the family. *Nada*."

She slumps down in her chair.

I reflect for a few moments and search for something comforting to say, finally, "As I said, seeing Jennifer and Jared at lacrosse tournaments and Jim cheering them on, the impression is they appear to be fine—happy, healthy and wholesome."

Sally breaks in, "And as I said, that's a facade. They have real problems and I'm not helping them. I'm in such a state of inertia. I'm just an appendage of Jim's. I have to defer, be demure and acquiesce. I'm not only letting myself down, I'm continually letting the kids down."

I wait for her to continue, she seems to have a need to spill out more. I suddenly am aware of the comforting scent of the soothing eucalyptus and bay leaves surrounding the deck. My hunched shoulders begin to relax.

"Listen to me, Sally. I've admired you so, your breeding and fine manners and sensitivity to others. I've also envied your wealth and glamorous lifestyle. You seem to have it all. Jim appears to adore you and to protect and treasure you. You all look so happy." I take her hand.

"Perhaps this will make it easier if you permit me to share my own personal story with you." She nods. "I never felt I had it together; my life was shattered by a sinister, quiet war with alcoholism. Talk about rage, you don't know the half of it. It drove me. Rage can do that, you know, as well as bring about the inertia you're experiencing."

I think back to those days of my own unremitting anger as I experienced the harrowing behavior of our own lop-sided lives. Remembering how I was always bracing myself for some kind of catastrophe, the unexpected happening, such as the unrelenting shame of that one unforgettable Thanksgiving Day and the turkey ending up on the floor with Todd's slurred remark, "Oh, the bird took flight."

While carving, he had lost his balance, due to too many pre-dinner cocktails. The turkey slid off the table. Of course, our friends stoically laughed and rushed to retrieve the spilled platter, but I was so angry.

And then a few weeks later during the December holidays, seeing the pain in Missy's eyes as she walked out into the living room Christmas morning and saw the Christmas tree shrunk into the size of a pygmy bonsai tree. Todd had been drinking the night before and had chosen to "shape it up" a bit.

Now, as I look back, these "happenings" appeared to others to have been humorous. To me, they were deeply embarrassing. We never knew what to expect. And I was always on guard, becoming alarmed whenever I sensed something disastrous might happen. I simply remembered being bone-tired, because I was always physically bracing myself for the next "event."

Sally moves closer to me on the wide redwood chaise and puts her arms around me.

"I am so sorry, Penny, I never suspected Todd's drinking was the cause of your troubles." She gently pats my shoulder as tears well up in my eyes.

"I was fighting against it daily. It was as if Todd was having an affair with the bottle. Alcohol was my competition. The doctors advised me to make a break. The effects of what was happening was damaging our health, mine and Missy's." I couldn't meet her eyes. "When I made the choice of removing the problem from our household, it was devastating. Everyday I live with the fact my decision to ask Todd to leave caused his death." I pause hesitantly, "Six months after he moved out and into that apartment, he died. He couldn't make it on his own without us." I begin to sob. "Your life seems so stable, look what happened to mine."

Sally reassuringly responds, "You made the best choice for you and Missy, Penny. Todd caused his own death. It wasn't due to your ultimatum."

"That's really not true! I didn't feel I had a choice. I felt the alcohol made the choice for me. I resented being forced into making that decision. Sally, you have a choice. I didn't."

"Hey, Penny, get real," she responds angrily. "What choice do I have? Leave? Come on. What am I going to do? A society dame who entertains!"

"There are lots of alternatives for you. You just haven't considered them, perhaps because you've been under such stress and you can't think straight."

"I'd jeopardize the kids' lifestyle. Do you think I'm going to risk that? Jim and I split up?" She shakes her head. "You know what that means, two households. In all divorces, the kids' education is the first to go. You think I'm going to allow that?"

I galvanize myself by taking a deep breath, "Okay, you might settle for what you have, but your kids will have to settle too. You've suggested Jennifer and Jared might have problems. Do you think the kids are happy, if you're so unhappy?"

"Oh, Penny, you know women of my status are conditioned not to show their emotions. To keep a stiff upper lip. The kids think I'm happy."

"I'm not so sure. You've just shared with me you've been seeking solace in napping and drinking. I'm sure the kids are aware of this, Sally. And from their viewpoint, from what they see, it might reflect poorly on you. The kids might not be aware of what you're truly going through."

I stare directly into those beautifully blue, but confused eyes.

"Well, yes, you might be right. I've been trying to cushion them and protect them. And I know Jared has been outwardly contemptuous of Jim lately. I sense he's aware something is going on. I'm finding he's very protective of me, which is sweet."

She shifts away from my direct gaze and says defensively, "You think Jim adores, treasures and protects me? Ha, what a joke." She rolls her eyes. "That's a myth. I'm one of his assets. And believe me, I have to earn my keep. After a few more of my snafus, and certainly after not showing up at our party tonight, Jim will make a move to get rid of me. If I continue to find solace in wine and sunsets and not meet the social obligations of being Mrs. Boothe, I guarantee, I will be given my walking papers." She shrugs, "In a way it's so easy, Jim will probably make the choice for me."

"Sally!"

She unexpectedly slams her wine glass down on the table and asserts, "And I'm not sure I'll be unhappy with that. I don't think I want to be his partner any more. I can't stand him. His goals have diametrically changed. When we started out, our lives were so lovely and simple. As the babies arrived, we were euphoric and then something inexplicable happened." She continues, "He changed slowly. For years I admired his entrepreneurial spirit, his charisma and ability to attract people. And at that time, he was devoted to us, even coached Jared's baseball team. But as time moved on, he became driven. So much for success."

She shivers and draws her hand-knit cabled cardigan around her thin shoulders. As the chilly fog creeps in over the hills, we sip our wine in silence, each of us lost in our own thoughts. We had shared our feelings long into the early morning hours. I am astonishingly surprised to learn we each had envied the other's life.

Later as I turn down the covers of Sally's bed in the small guest room, I stare into the dresser mirror and think Sally and I are alike after all. I begrudgingly have to admit neither of us is making choices for ourselves. We are traditional fifties women. All our lives, we have been accustomed to our parents and husbands making our decisions. How would we know how to go about deciding? Alcohol very forcefully finally made my decision. And it appears Sally will allow Jim to make hers.

* * * * *

The following morning we sit out on the deck drinking French roast coffee. The phone rings.

"Please, don't pick up, Penny," pleads Sally. "Let it be. I know it must be Jim. We communicate only through answering machines these days. Rather sad, isn't it."

The message machine plays out.

"Sally, I know you're there. Chancie told me where you were. Your act last night was the ultimate. Mimi Wood was very pointedly inquiring about your where-abouts. And Dan Wood expressed the fact your absence was worrying." He pauses, "What was I to say? You're not being here signaled something was wrong. They want to invest in a sure thing. They want to see stability. They're accustomed to husbands and wives working as a team. You blew it Sally, you lost the deal!" There is another longer pause, "I'm sorry to break this to you on the answering machine Sal, but later this morning I'm going to call Harry and ask him to draw up divorce papers. We've both discussed this step in the past, so I know this isn't coming as a surprise to you."

"It's over," she whispers.

Shocked into silence, we sit and stare at each other. We listen to the bubbling of the creek as it trickles down the mountain making its way through the redwoods to the bucolic meadow. If a neighbor had viewed the scene, they might surmise here are two women serenely starting their day on a redwood deck without a care in the world, leisurely enjoying their morning croissants, coffee and pleasant conversation.

The Alley

Jennifer's Story

Something is wrong; the fog horns are keeping her awake tonight. Usually they lull Jennifer to sleep as she hums along to their comforting sounds. The tinkling of the bells on the buoys across the San Francisco Bay softly join in with the steady rhythm of the horns. These same buoys are a life raft for seals, who lounge upon them seeking refuge from trawlers and mighty international tankers as they plow across the surface of the waters to their destinations. Through the night the seals engage in raucous barking at each other, creating a musical cacophony of sounds, which ricochet from shore to shore. But this evening instead of finding solace in these soothing lullabies, the effects of this natural chorus seems to be keeping Jennifer awake for hours. Maybe it's because she's so wound up from today's activities. She can't think of any other reason.

She and her best friend, Trisha, both juniors at Marin Academy, decided to go over to downtown Mill Valley. They had an awesome afternoon watching the guys on their skateboards at the outdoor bus depot. As they sat on the benches under the tall redwoods surrounding the outdoor plaza, they shrieked with delight when one of the skateboarders would take a huge gamble and collapse in a heap on the pavement. After hearing the girls' approval, the grinning boys revved up and took even greater risks. Part of the plaza was in step-stone tiers and as they began their clickety, clackety descent from the top tier, the risk of taking a disastrous tumble lurked in the back of viewers' minds.

After awhile, the girls grew bored by this entertainment and Trish suggested, "Let's bop over to Banana Republic on Throckmorton. Their clothes are so rad."

"Okay, but as far as I'm concerned, trying on clothes is my least favorite thing to do these days," responded Jennifer.

As they entered the brightly lit store filled with the latest early 1970s designer sportswear, Trisha spied a colorful blouse. She hauled it off the rack and held it up to herself. "Hey, look at this awesome Cacherel blouse, Jen. This is in your favorite color. Isn't the blue floral print cool?" As Trish searched through the racks of warm, sunny California colors, they realized there really wasn't anything above a size four in that particular blouse, nor in most of the blouses.

Jen was crestfallen.

"Please, don't put on that face," Trish admonished. "Lighten up. No one could fit into most of these clothes. I think it's funny, don't you? They only have clothes for emaciated women. Gee, if you think you'd have trouble getting into this blouse think of me. I'm a size eight."

Still, Jen had been mortified. Returning home she discovered the rest of the family was out. Good, she thought as she raced up the stairs to her bedroom. She got on the treadmill. The others wouldn't know how long she'd been on it. If she lost a few pounds, she could fit into those size fours. She switched on the machine, setting the speed to the optimum level. She didn't think Mom kept track of her time on it anyway, but just in case, she'd secretly get as much of a workout before they all returned home for dinner.

Why did she have to be so obese? Why couldn't she reduce the size of her thighs? If her leg muscles got any larger from swim practice, she'd have to drop out. That's for sure! Forget about loving the feeling of speeding through water. Forget about winning.

She remembered Trish telling her she looked so cool in the new team swimsuit. But she knew differently. Sometimes, she felt like one of those beached whales off of the Sonoma coast. Swimming was making her body larger for God's sake.

The other day at the pool, as they awaited their turn, she noticed Mrs. Whitney eaves-dropping on them. She and Trisha were talking about their weight after they had done laps.

Mrs. Whitney interrupted their conversation with, "Jen, you haven't lost any more weight have you? You need that weight for energy and endurance. Don't think being smaller will move you through the water faster." She shook her finger at Jen, "After practice I want to meet you in the changing room at the scale. If you don't maintain at least the weight you have, I'll have to take you off the team. I can't risk you ruining your health by having you become too thin."

Jen shrugged. My gosh, that woman was actually shaking her finger at her. How rude! That loony old lady.

Why was she so darned concerned about weight? What about her own weight?

Still, she was fond of Mrs. Whitney, especially when she enveloped her in a huge bear hug after a major win. She was so plump and motherly and soft. Mom never hugged like that. Of course, her mom was pencil thin, so when she hugged, Jen inexplicably drew away. She became so disconcerted. All she could feel were her mother's bones.

On the way home that afternoon when she became so unhappy about not being able to fit into the size four at Banana Republic, she suggested to Trisha they buy hair dye in order to compensate. It's time for a radical change, she had stated. Trisha, her soul mate, was game for anything. She chose strawberry blonde and Jennifer a soft purple.

Well, at last, her sleepless night is at an end. The sun is rising over the East Bay hills. She'll try the hair dye this morning. As she enters her cluttered bathroom, she first hops on the scale. Oh God, a quarter of a pound. It's over 104. Higher than the day before, when Mrs. Whitney had weighed her. Disaster city. In despair she grabs the tube of purple dye and enters the shower. When she glances out at the mirror, she notices the dye has drizzled down over her body. That won't do, she giggles. She scrubs herself furiously. As the blow dryer drones on, she peeks at the mirror and is infinitely pleased. A really rad look. Wow, she looks so awesome, there are so many varying shades of purple; streaks of magenta, thin strands of violet, slivers of lilac, fuchsia and lavender coiling about her head.

The Alley

Throwing on her jeans, a tee, a denim jacket, and tying a red madras scarf around her neck, she rechecks the mirror. Good, no one will notice her ugly shape. Her hair will surely draw attention away from what is happening. Getting past Dad though will be a problem, but only momentarily: he could at certain times be such a softie.

Clattering downstairs and entering the kitchen she quickly heads for the fridge. Maybe they won't notice. Dad is reading the sports pages in the *San Francisco Chronicle* and Mom is lost in her knitting and nibbling raspberries. Jennifer pours a tiny bit of cranberry juice in her cup and heads for the long cherry side-board. Mom has made bran muffins.

Better get it over with. She turns to face them, "Good morning."

Both look up. Not surprisingly, their morning smiles vanish instantly.

Jim groans, "My God, Sally, look what that kid has done. Can't you control your children? One looks like Jerry Garcia and the other is suddenly becoming Cher. How much self-expression do we foster in this household?"

"Oh, Jim, don't take them so seriously. It's just a stage they're going through."

"For God's sake, Sally, I was planning on introducing them to our guests at the party tomorrow night. Fat chance. Jennifer, sweetheart, how can you do this to me?"

"Oh, Dad, I think it looks cool. Don't stress. Listen to Mom."

Sally suddenly looks up from her knitting and glows

at Jennifer. Jennifer smiles, thinking, so rarely do she and her mom smile at each other. They're usually engaged in their proverbial mother/daughter warfare.

Her dad scrutinizes Jen again, grins and then returns to his newspaper.

Moving out on to the redwood deck, which spans the multi-tiered mansion, she surreptitiously edges toward the bird feeder. Her trusty finches will save her again. She checks to see if she's being watched. No, it's safe.

Crumpling her bran muffin on to their feeding tray, she whispers, "There my dear friends. I'll take care of you, and you'll take care of me."

She paces back and forth along the lengthy, encompassing deck, pretending to look at the wide-ranging views of the bay. It appears a fleet of sloops from the Corinthian Yacht Club is forming off Angel Island, preparing for the starting gun. What a beautiful day. The sun is sparkling on the water. It flashes off the windows of the huge towers of commerce in downtown San Francisco. She lives in the best possible of all worlds. Why then is she so dissatisfied, especially with herself? Her pacing becomes more intense. Sometimes she can't help it. It's as if someone else is in control. She thinks back to when she forced herself to always keep moving. Now, she can't seem to stop. She wonders if anyone else notices.

Jared pokes his head out the sliding door.

"What are you doing? You act like you've got St. Vitus Dance."

"I'm just watching what's going on out on the bay."

"Oh, yeah, right. Every morning you're moving over this deck at eighty miles an hour. It doesn't give you much time for viewing. What's the point?"

"I'm in a hurry, so what's it to you? Mind your own business!"

"You're weird, Jen!"

Maybe Jared was on to her. But now she has to get back through the kitchen without too much parental trauma. She hurriedly shoves past her brother, moving through the sliding door and edges towards the hallway.

"Did you enjoy my bran muffins, Jen? Did you drink your cranberry juice?"

"Yes, the muffin was scrumptious, and I did finish my juice."

"I thought you'd notice the hint of lemon I put in the muffins, could you taste it? Do you think it added to their flavor? Bran muffins can be so bland."

For a moment Jen is taken aback, why is Mom quizzing her about breakfast? "There is something deliciously different about them, Mom, just couldn't put my finger on it."

She sails out the door, grabbing her backpack on the hallway chair and slams the front redwood door behind her. Out in front of the house she looks up the lane for Mrs. Paige, who is carpooling today. As she waits she paces up and down the wide lavender-lined driveway. She is greeted by the soothing, soft scent of the tiny purple buds on the tall stalks. Continuing up and down, up and down, back and forth, pacing as fast as she can, she notices gorgeous Bart Green across the way edging his Jeep Cherokee out of the driveway. She waves.

He revs up the motor and draws the Jeep up close.

He stares at her in bewilderment, "Hey, Jen, Jeez,

what did you do to your hair? You were my blondie, my Goldie Hawn. What the heck happened?"

"I just needed a change."

"Well purple hair is sure a change. Do you want a ride to school?"

"No thanks, I'd better wait for Mrs. Paige, she's expecting to pick me up."

He frowns and shakes his head, "When are you going to give me a break? I stop by every morning. Can't you ride with me just this once?"

She smiles. "Sometime soon, Bart, when I remember to let Mrs. Paige know ahead of time."

"How about tomorrow? Tell her you're driving with me tomorrow."

"We'll see. I'll try to arrange it."

As he pulls away, she suddenly becomes aware she has consented to Bart's invitation. She grows anxious. She doesn't want to get too close to Bart. She doesn't want him touching her fat, pudgy body. She'll call him tonight and tell him her dad insisted Mrs. Paige drive her to school.

The familiar old Mercedes diesel roars up the hill. Jennifer jumps in. Grinning at Trisha, she gives her a high five when she sees her brightly tinted strawberry blonde hair. Mrs. Paige is so cool, she has the Tasmanian Devils on the car stereo. No one needs to make conversation. Driving up the freeway and over the Kentfield grade is an unusually calm journey this morning; Trisha and her Mom are argument-free.

As Mrs. Paige pulls into the Marin Academy parking lot, she smiles conspiratorially, "That's an unusually attractive do, Jen."

Jennifer grins. Mrs. Paige always made her feel so good about herself.

As the diesel pulls away, Trisha turns and says, "Can you beat that? I don't get her. She always says such nice things to you. But as far as I'm concerned, boy, did I get it this morning. Would you believe that woman threw me in the shower and tried to rinse this rad color out of my hair? I was yelling and screaming. The Woods—you know the neighbors next door—even called to see if everything was all right."

Jen giggles, "Oh, don't worry about it, Trish. She's just your mom, she'll get over it."

They hit Bill Strang's creative writing class. He is so cool; an awesome dude as far as the kids are concerned. Is it any wonder? He really understands them. And he listens to them, actually listens. But Jen had heard the new headmaster, Mr. Goodwin, didn't approve of him.

She recently discovered this when she eavesdropped on a conversation between her parents about Marin Academy and whether they were going to make a huge donation this year. Her father said there was a change in the air. The trustees had forced the old headmaster, Mr. Whitney, out, feeling he wasn't aggressive enough in getting the Marin Academy kids placed in elite Eastern colleges.

She grins to herself as she remembers back to the time when the kids had to initially adjust to the new headmaster. It was hilarious, the graduation ceremony. A new headmaster, Bruce Goodman, was in charge; graduation being his first major event at Marin Academy. All the kids knew he wanted to make a good impression on the parents. There he was in his official capacity, standing in a pin-striped suit in the warm early afternoon sun, waiting for the graduates to emerge over the crest of the hill. Jen was seated with her parents at the edge of the meadow under the huge leafy maples shading them from the June sunshine. Some of Jen's friends from the upper class were graduating, so she had wanted to attend. And her dad, of course, wanted to be there for business connections.

The school band began playing *Pomp and Circumstance*. As the graduating class made its way down the gently sloping hill, parents glowingly nudged each other. Their kids appeared to look like normal people. Jen and the lower classes felt betrayed as they saw guys dressed in traditional navy blue blazers with rep ties and khaki pants, and girls in flowery Liberty of London print dresses. The lower class was becoming suspicious and murmurs of dissent could be heard. What had happened? In the past, graduation had been a time to express unconventionality in what they chose to wear. They attempted to emulate the pioneer wagon train look of long calico dresses and Cochise-like garb or wore Indian saris or peacenik attire. As the graduates drew nearer however, the audience broke into laughter. The seniors took their places in the assigned bleachers facing their families. Why the inexplicable laughter from the viewers? One item in the big picture was missing. None of the graduating class wore shoes.

Mr. Goodwin's face was flushed crimson with rage. The Boothes' mutual friend, Chancie Paige, was sitting with Jennifer's family. She was shaking with laughter.

Chancie turned and grinned at Sally, saying, "They still have their high spirits, don't they? You can't drum that out of them."

* * * * *

Awesome Bill Strang is passing out their short stories as they leave the classroom. Sandy-haired, blue-eyed Bill stands at Jennifer's desk. He is so preppy, dressed in chinos, a Glen-plaid shirt and L. L. Bean moccasins. Searching intently among the papers, he flicks through them as fast as he can. Students are sneaking out the door attempting to avoid the fait accompli of a D, or worse, written across the top of their papers. Bart Green speeds towards the door giving her a high five and makes a hasty exit. Jen's not certain she'd like to see her paper either. As Bill stands between their desks, Trisha gives him an adoring look, never letting her eyes leave his face. She doesn't care what she gets for a grade, Jen thinks. This is just an excuse for Trisha to stand next to him. Jen doesn't know whether to be disgusted or amused. With a sweeping flourish Bill finally hands Trisha her paper. Jen sees a B+. Trisha doesn't seem concerned with the grade, in fact, she continues grinning at Bill. Gosh, Jen thinks, if I got a B+, I'd be devastated. Finally he turns and leans down to show Jen her paper. She sees an A. She scans the written comments. She is crushed. She falters as she gathers her books and rises to leave.

"What Jennifer, you unhappy with an A again? You know you're the only student in my creative writing classes who consistently gets A's and is consistently unhappy about it. What's the deal?"

"Every time I see your hand written comments, I freak out. I think there must be something wrong. My writing is just drivel, anyway."

"Jen, my hand-written notes are all positives. You're not processing the comments correctly. You're mixing up what I'm writing on your papers. You are a gifted writer. Do you hear what I'm saying. You're a gifted writer!"

"No, the descriptive phrases of nature in my pieces are too long and the dialogue seems stilted at times. I'll never get it all right."

Bill leans closer and stares directly into her eyes, "Take it from me, Jennifer, it's the best writing, I've ever seen. Do you hear me? Do you get it?'

Jen nods and inches away quickly. She edges toward the door. Bill's stern voice has made her uncomfortable. It's definitely time to make a run to the bagel shop. She rushes down the hill toward Fourth Street and walks into the alley entering the shop through the back door.

"The usual, Missy?"

"Yes, please."

She hastily digs in her pocket for a ten dollar bill. The anxiety is too much.

Quickly she carries the bagels back out to the alley, and stands behind the stacks of garbage cans. Eating with great haste, she scarfs down six large bagels as fast as she can. As she waits, she paces. Why did Bill Strang speak to her so sternly? The sound of his voice terrified her. When will she ever please him? When is she ever going to please anyone? Her work sucks. She sucks. She can't do anything right. The anxiety begins to slowly dissipate. She finds an empty garbage can and sticks her finger down her throat.

After the first wave passes, she pauses and looks up, she thinks she sees Mrs. Whitney's shadow at the end of the alley. Oh great. That's just great. She can't look back to check whether Mrs. Whitney is still watching; more is coming up. She leans over the can. After a few moments, she senses the change. She is calm now and at peace, the anxiety has disappeared. She pops a piece of gum in her mouth to hide the hideous smell. She pats down her hair and straightens her blouse, checks to see if there are any telltale stains on her skirt. She walks calmly up the grassy slope towards campus.

* * * * *

While Jen is in the alley, her parents, Sally and Jim, are a few blocks away waiting in the headmaster's foyer on campus.

"The Boothes, two of my most favorite people," Bruce Goodman gushes as he ushers them into his softly lit office. The dim lighting offers a sense of ease and gentility.

Jim Boothe silently thinks Goodman better greet them affably, after all, they had donated a tidy sum to last year's building campaign. He glances about the office at the wood paneling, plush wool carpet and huge library of books lining the walls. Jim had been told Goodman was bookish. That is suspect at best, but why did this guy insist upon having this office redecorated? He'd ask the trustees about it.

He watches Goodman smile appreciatively at Sally as

she makes her way toward one of the Hitchcock chairs in front of his desk. Sally is smiling demurely at him. Goodman grins back in seemingly awed silence. Her beauty seems to have stunned him into muteness. She is dressed in a powder blue cashmere sweater set that enhances those sparkling blue eyes. Abruptly the office door swings open and Laura Whitney and Bill Strang enter.

"Sorry we're late, headmaster." They both ease into the chintz love seat against the far wall, somewhat out of range seemingly uniting themselves as one unit.

The Boothes direct their bewildered looks at the headmaster.

He leans forward and smiles at them both reassuringly.

He begins, Jim notices with a somewhat placating tone. "I've asked Laura Whitney and Bill Strang to take part in our little discussion this afternoon. They're very familiar with Jennifer and her skills. Laura takes great pride in Jennifer's swimming accomplishments and Bill is extremely proud of your daughter's writing abilities.

He shifts back into his chair, "They are both recommending her for a full scholarship at UCLA. As you know, that university has an outstanding swim team known internationally and also by the way, it has a creative writing program comparable to Columbia University back east."

"Just a minute, we hadn't been made aware anyone else would be attending this session," says Jim.

Sally frowns, saying, "I thought we were here to simply fill out preliminary papers. I thought we were going to just discuss the possibility of Jennifer receiving an academic scholarship in creative writing for an eastern college."

"Yes, I just mentioned Mrs. Whitney and Mr. Strang are going to sign the papers recommending Jen receive a scholarship. We're going to do that, but before we do, Bill Strang thought we'd better address a few other issues with you that seem to be impacting Jennifer's performance. We're concerned about her future far away from home next year. We are recommending she choose an institution closer to home."

Jim fumes. What's going on here? What's this upstart, Strang up to? And UCLA—over my dead body. Jim twists himself in his chair, so he is directly facing Bill and Laura. Meet the enemy head on that's what he always says.

There are a few moments of silence in the office. They can hear the carillon playing in the bell tower outside. Sally begins to fidget with her pearls. Jim is hoisting himself up to his full six feet two inches, readying himself to get to the bottom of this. He appears to be bracing to do battle. Bruce Goodman hesitates and then begins.

"Sally and Jim, as you are well aware, here at Marin Academy we are interested in the whole student. I know you are aware we've been able to keep the ratio between faculty and student at ten to one, which produces a closeness not found at other schools. The faculty feels we function as a surrogate family to these kids."

He leans forward, "Since there is this desired closeness, recently we've become a bit concerned about Jennifer's health. She's become increasingly thin and appears to be disguising it with layers of clothes."

They all hear a slight gasp from Sally.

He turns toward Laura Whitney. "Mrs. Whitney would you like to share your observations with the Boothes?"

"Jim and Sally, I have noticed at swim practice when I weigh the team members that Jen has lost an enormous amount of weight and it has been of concern to me over the past few months. Also, something came up, just a few moments ago, that I am terribly concerned about. I was alarmed to see Jen in the alley behind the Bagel Shop on Fourth Street. She was throwing up into a garbage can."

Sally edges forward almost out of her chair toward Laura, "How disgusting. What do you mean Jen was throwing up in the alley? It had to be another student. You're mistaken."

"She was throwing up in the garbage cans; it appeared she was holding a large empty paper bag for bagels."

"Laura, dear, I'm trying to understand why you would say such a thing. We consider you our very dear friend, why I remember when we all set up this academy together for the kids. we all became so close. I'm sure you've made an error."

As she continues she begins to wring her hands, something Jim had never seen her do before. "You know Jennifer is such a lady and I know we both couldn't imagine her doing something like that, throwing up in a garbage can out in public. It's simply preposterous."

Laura stares apprehensively at Sally.

"It was definitely Jen, she's lost a lot of weight lately

Sally, I'm sure you've noticed."

"Well, if you wouldn't push the kid so hard in swim practice, she wouldn't lose so much weight. She probably has to stuff herself, because of all the laps you make her do," retorts Jim sharply.

Laura blurts out, "Jim, we're not concerned about her stuffing herself, we're concerned about her throwing up and becoming emaciated."

Laura turns and with her elbow nudges Bill Strang sitting next to her. Jim notes she seems to be beseeching him to make his comments and back her up.

Finally, Bill draws himself up and in a calm voice begins, "Mr. and Mrs. Boothe, the younger faculty members are worried about Jen. It's not only her weight; it's her thinking processes, her negative repetitive thoughts about herself and her low self-esteem. We're really concerned about her well-being. She receives the best grades of all the students in all my classes, and she's still not satisfied with her work, nor with herself. We feel it's imperative to bring this to your attention. You must realize something is amiss with Jen."

At this Jim shoots back, "You're telling me there's something wrong with my daughter. Listen, we're good parents. We would have noticed it. We're close to our kids." He shakes his finger at Strang, "Don't tell me about my daughter, she's my daughter, not your's. You stick to helping her get good grades, that's your job. And none of this crap you've been feeding her about UCLA. She's going to an eastern school, an Ivy League school."

Undeterred Bill continues, "Mr. Boothe, look, we brought you in here because of our concern for Jennifer and her mental, emotional and physical state. You don't seem to be receiving these comments as well as we expected. We want to work closely with you both for Jennifer's sake. We think there is a need for her to be placed in therapy."

"I don't have to listen to this guy, Goodman. What does he know? He's a sixties radical. He's almost a Communist, a Leftie. He's getting the kids all stirred up in class reading Trotsky and things like that."

Bruce Goodman shifts forward in his Windsor chair and says, "Now, Jim, Bill is a fine teacher and the kids all really relate to him. In fact, to be honest with you, they love him. They genuinely sense he cares for each of them. He's drawn an enormous amount of creativity out of them. We've had many of his students publish their work in national literary reviews. And you know as well as I, that's good for the school simply because of the publicity angle. I mean where else have you heard of a prep school student publishing in a national review?"

"He's going where he shouldn't go. I'm warning you. What he's focusing upon is a family matter and he's gone over the boundaries."

The headmaster placatingly suggests, "Ask Jen how much she's learning from him. Perhaps you'd better consult your own daughter about this."

At this remark, Jim rises suddenly. "Come on, Sally, I don't want to listen to this. I don't want to be reminded of when I should consult my daughter. Let's go home. We'll deal with this ourselves if we deal with it at all. I'm tired of hearing all of this nonsense about my daughter's well-being."

Sally rises in quiet submission. She appears to be tremoring, but her face is serene. She makes her way to the paneled door, but then turns and never forgetting her good manners, she shakes Bill's hand.

"Mr. Strang, I know you are interested in Jennifer's welfare. She just loves you." She smiles. "But to be honest with you, I haven't heard Jennifer make any negative comments about herself and too, I think Laura might have made an innocent error about Jen's weight. Why, you know how all we women are about our weight. Look at me, I'm constantly dieting. I'm going to think about what you've told us, but I'm sure you're mistaken."

As Sally eases out the door, she suggests, "Laura, why don't you and Jack come over for wine and brie next Friday? We miss seeing you both."

Laura and Bill simply stare after her in astonishment.

After the door is closed, Laura turns to both men, "She's not going to acknowledge any of this. They are both in denial. I'm really worried about Jen. What are we to do?"

"We did our best," remarks Bruce Goodman. He looks out the window and watches Jim ease his silver shadow Jaguar out of the reserved parking space and murmurs, "I wonder if this means we will be losing the hefty annual Boothe donation?"

* * * * *

Jennifer is in a fog. It's misty like the San Francisco Bay fog. Except she can't hear the sounds of the seals, horns and buoys. The light is becoming clearer, it's beginning to become brighter too. And it's so noisy. There is a sharp clanging of steel equipment. There is a beeping. She can hear muffled voices issuing orders.

"Her potassium rate is really low. We've got to bring it up and steady it."

"Her electrolytes are way off. We need to get her stabilized."

Jen hears her mom quietly sobbing. She's pleading, "Please, someone tell me, is she going to be all right?"

"Ma'am, how long do you think your daughter has been unconscious?"

Jen hears her mother respond, "I have no idea. She hadn't come down for breakfast, so I went up to get her. I found her on the floor next to her treadmill. It was still running."

"Do you know how long the treadmill was on, ma'am? Did you hear it going all night?"

"No, I don't know. Earlier in the evening, I had a few glasses of wine. I was out on the deck and heard Mr. Boothe ordering Jen to eat two helpings of dinner. She seemed to sit at the table for at least an hour trying to consume the food. Then she went upstairs and I heard the treadmill go on."

Jim interjects, "Now, Sally, we don't need to go into all those details of last evening."

"I just wanted to answer the assistant's question, Jim."

"You've been helpful, Mrs. Boothe."

Jen hears her mom whimper, "I really don't know exactly what time the treadmill went on."

"That's okay, ma'am, we'll do our best to stabilize her."

She hears her dad's shout, "Well, please, please do something. It appears my daughter is growing weaker.

Why are you questioning my wife? This isn't time for conversation. We need action right now, not questions. Help my baby girl for God sakes."

As the machines register different sounds, Jen hears her dad begging, "Please I'm sorry I lost it, hurry, please hurry, she's sinking." Strange, she's never heard her dad use that tone before. He's usually always so demanding of others.

She hears an authoritative voice, "Sir, we're doing all we can. Could you both please wait in the hallway, we think it best right now. We have to administer various medications and shift some equipment around. We'll call you back a little later."

Jen feels a pat on her shoulder, "Jen, dear, we'll be right outside the door."

She attempts to take her mom's hand, but something is holding her back. She's covered tightly in a sheet.

It is growing quieter. She struggles to focus on what people are saying, but their voices are getting softer. Is she in a hospital? The voices fade. She's so tired. She drifts off again. She can hear the fog horns and the tinkling buoys. She smiles. She thinks she can hear the seals barking to each other. She hums along softly to the comforting sounds as the light in the room seems to be getting softer and softer. She feels peaceful. Suddenly there's a ray of light, it seems to be beckoning to her. She wants to follow it.

Buddies at the Bonfire

Jared's Story

Jared's guilty feelings have lessened considerably. The beer is beginning to have its effect. They had struggled to tap the keg, but it had careened across the sand down toward the shoreline several times. A cheer finally went up when they were able to get it upright. A few drops of the stuff actually emerged from the hose. They had been drinking now for at least an hour.

Kevin pipes up, "You know what, you guys? I dig you more than I do my own family."

"Yeah, me too. I don't understand anyone in my family. My old man is really down on me," adds Jared. "We'll never be able to get along. He hates me."

"Nah," interjects Sam, "Our dads just don't know where we're coming from, that's all. They just don't dig us. But they sure as hell don't have to be so nasty about everything we do."

"I don't know why my dad is so mad. He's mad at every friggin' thing and every friggin' body. Boy, when he comes home from work, he's a raving maniac," Richie complains.

"They're crazy, you all know that," says Jared. "Sometimes I get so mad at my old man, I want to sock him. We almost duked it out last weekend."

"Hey you guys, we're having a good time here at the beach. Let's forget about those old pissers, okay? Forget what's happening back over the hill where we live. This is the Buddy Bonfire, remember. I'm going to pass out some joints. Maybe that will mellow us out and help us forget about dads," advises Kevin. There is hooting and hollering. This is the first time they have smoked grass. "Would you believe I was able to get the weed from a guy selling it on the edge of campus."

The surf laps quietly against the shoreline. As the fog edges up the beach, the sky becomes murky. One can barely see the lights atop the Golden Gate Bridge. The fog horns triggered by a technical mechanism begin to bellow in unison. It is the mid seventies and modern technology has created a symphony of sounds across the bay. A chill sets in. The boys inch closer together. Zipping up their jackets, they hover near the warm flames of the fire.

They pass the joints from one to another. After twenty minutes, the marijuana is beginning to have its desired effect. Jared thinks smoking pot is awesome. He's never had it before. He feels an inordinate sense of camaraderie with his buddies. They are a real team—them against the world—and especially against their parents. This is a groovy idea, meeting here every Friday night at Muir Beach for the Buddy Bonfire. He's glad they're not talking about their dads anymore.

"Let's talk about chicks," he suggests. Uncontrollable snickering follows.

"Yeah Jared, as if you'd know what to do with chicks."

"I know all right. Don't underestimate me."

"Okay, then tell us."

"Well, you get a little feel in first."

"Then what."

Silence. Then, lots of guffaws.

"He doesn't know what's next. Jared doesn't know what's next."

Richie comes to his rescue by putting a tape in the boom box. They all smile. It's their song. They begin to softly whistle the theme from "The Bridge on the River Kwai," which drifts over the sand and out to sea.

Jared stares out at the Pacific and listens to the surf. He loves the shore, remembering the times his family took a house for a month over at Stinson Beach. That was really cool. He reminisces about searching for sea shells and digging pits with shovels in the sand, hoping to get to China. And the afternoon break of leaving the beach and going to the Dairy Dip to get a frostie. It was one of the few times when they seemed normal and no one argued. They'd get up in the morning and while having breakfast watch the seals play tag in the lagoon. Mid-morning they'd go clamming or fishing, so Mom could make a choppino stew that night. Mostly they would just mess around. After dinner they'd have these giant Monopoly contests. His mom would laugh so hard she'd have to rush to the john every ten minutes. When was the last time Mom had that much fun? She was so pretty when she laughed like that. Lately her face was so tight and tense; once he even thought he heard her grinding her teeth for God's sake. She and the old man were locked in mortal combat these days. Or else, she was dopey from her chardonnay.

Trying not to think about it, he concentrates on the sounds of the surf and the rhythm of the waves. The tides are really beginning to churn as the sky darkens. He can't even see the stars, the fog has done its filtering job.

* * * * *

As the Bonfire Buddies mellow out, over on the other side of Mount Tamalpais, two deputies receive a request from dispatch about an out-of-control fire at Muir Beach. The neighbors in the summer cottages on the hill have reported a huge blaze down close to the shoreline. Deputies Steven Walsh and Glen Thomas had just taken their coffee break at the café in Tam Junction. They had started out together at cadet academy and after twelve years in detentions had built up a real friendship. Now they are assigned to patrol West Marin. As they pay their bill and leave the café, both check the weather; fog is coming in.

Slowly proceeding in their respective patrol cars over Mt. Tamalpais toward Muir Beach, they rise over the crest of the final hill and can see the huge fire with figures huddled around it. They radio each other and decide to approach with lights dimmed. If it is just a matter of an overly large bonfire having to be doused, they don't want to cause a major event with squad car lights flashing and sirens screeching. After all, this is Marin and one did his best not to upset the natives. Incidents had to be handled with discretion or there'd be political problems. They'd hauled in too many wealthy VIPs for DUIs and then gotten hell for it. It was well-known throughout the Bay Area that law enforcement was a custodial matter in Marin. Everyone applied for a position there, since it was a relatively safe gig. There was so little real crime, except for drug busts.

Both of them ease their cars down the dirt road toward the beach. It appears the figures around the fire are not alarmed by the size of the blaze, in fact they are adding more driftwood to it. Probably crazy teenagers. Walsh and Thomas notice a green Land Rover hidden at the edge of the nearby lot and radio the vehicle's license plate numbers into dispatch, sensing they'd better learn as much as they can. They park their patrol cars at the trailhead and stealthily move down the sandy path towards the fire. As they draw close they smell the all too sweet familiar aroma. Marijuana.

Thomas signals Walsh. They each approach from the northwest and southwest respectively in order to corner the culprits. Though it is pitch dark they are able to keep track of each others' movements. Walsh waits for Thomas to signal.

* * * * *

Jared smiles; the buddies are pretty mellow now. A few moments ago they had gotten into an argument about whether to add more logs to the fire. Kevin is so stoked, he wants a sky-high blaze. The rest of them don't want to attract attention, but Kevin rules the night. After all he is the pot supplier.

Hearing the snap of a branch toward the north, Jared looks up the beach to check it out.

"Hey, did you guys hear something? Turn that tape off for a second."

He sees no one.

Kevin taunts, "Jared's getting paranoid. Loosen up, dude."

Suddenly the deputies are upon them. They race out of the shadows, their high beam flashlights blinding the boys, who are toppling into one another as they quickly rise.

"Just stay put," orders Deputy Thomas.

Richie, Kevin, Bob and Joe streak off in an easterly direction uphill towards the dense grove of redwoods. All are members of the track team and they fly. Deputy Walsh takes off in hot pursuit. He doesn't draw his gun. These are kids. At first Walsh follows them closely on foot, but after a few grueling minutes, loses the teenagers as they disappear into the thickly ferned redwood forest. Realizing he'll never catch up to them over that ridge, he makes his way back to the campfire.

Because Thomas has seen the others take off, he has chosen to draw his gun. He wants to intimidate Jared and Sam to keep them in place.

"Okay you two, give your names, ages and where you live."

The boys turn ashen at the sight of the weapon.

"Jared Boothe, sir, I'm fourteen and I live at 430 Belvedere Way."

"Sam Meehan, sir, I'm fourteen and live at 22 Tiburon Lane." Deputy Thomas shakes his head and shouts out to Walsh who is stumbling back through the brush, "They're just kids, Walsh." He holsters his gun.

Jared glances at Deputy Thomas. He must be 6'4" and weigh 240 pounds, a huge guy. He wonders why the deputy pulled a gun. It sure gave him a heck of a shock. He guessed that's why the deputy did it.

Sam is shaking so hard, they can hear his teeth chatter. Jared puts his arm around his buddy's shoulders for a second to try to calm him down.

"Now you guys know you're breaking the law, right? We could smell the marijuana half way down the path. Where'd you get it?" demands Thomas.

Both boys shrug.

"You'd better make it easier on yourselves, this is serious business."

"A friend got it for us."

"Yeah, what's his name?'

Neither of them were going to squeal on Kevin.

Jared finally responds. "Sir, our friend got it for us on the edge of campus at Marin Academy."

Thomas says, "It is well known in the county the drug pushers have staked out that area. They know you rich kids have the bread at Marin Academy. What are you, freshman?"

"Yes, sir."

Deputy Walsh finally appears out of the dark. He is breathing heavily and sighs ruefully, "I lost them, Glen, they are like rabbits, they are so fast. They separated and disappeared over the ridge into the redwoods."

He leans over gasping for breath, his heaviness has sorely been tested.

"Boys, you sure have loyal friends, who stick by you," announces Walsh. "And I'll bet the so-called friend who bought the pot is one of the ones who disappeared over the hill. Some friend. Left you to take the rap."

Jared and Sam pale. Sam's legs are shaking uncontrollably.

Deputy Thomas asks, "Ever done pot before?'

"No sir," in unison.

He looks at Walsh, "Let's have these guys put out the fire with those empty trash cans." He glares at the boys, "You guys, fill those cans with water from the ocean and drag them up here to the fire. I don't care whether you bust your backs or how many trips it takes. Just do it. Get moving."

While the boys trudge back and forth, Jared overhears the deputies discussing the situation.

"Steve, even though they broke the law, smoking pot and stuff, they're just kids. From what they tell me this is their first time. We might get our butts kicked in if their parents raise a big stink."

"I agree it seems like a goddarn shame to take them in. I ran their names into dispatch. There's no record or anything on them. We could get our asses whipped if we do bring them in. He shakes his head, saying, "But they did commit a misdemeanor."

"Why not let this one ride with a strong warning to them and their parents?"

"I'm okay with that," says Thomas. "But, I sure hate talking to parents. They're bound to give us a hard time. I'd rather explain the situation to the booking sergeant than a parent. If we charge them, the kids will have to wait out court time in juvenile detention, which since they haven't had any priors would be really tough. You and I know being in detentions makes them worse." He instructs, "Call dispatch and tell them the bonfire is out.

We're escorting two teenage kids home. Don't mention the marijuana to the dispatcher right now. We'll include that in our written reports with 'suspicion of marijuana.' Have the Land Rover towed. That should cost one of the parents a pretty penny."

The fire is out and Jared's and Sam's faces are becoming green from the after effects of the pot and the exertion of hauling trash cans filled with sea water up the beach. They've overheard some of the conversation between the deputies and are hoping they'll be able to get out of this mess.

The deputies signal them to move up the path to the squad cars. The roar of the thundering surf follows as they trudge up the dirt lane. As time has passed the tides have moved up the beach and now encroach upon the shrinking shoreline. The residue from the buddies' bonfire is slipping out to sea.

"Get in the car," Deputy Thomas instructs Jared.

"You, do the same," says Deputy Walsh to Sam.

Jared looks back at Sam huddled in the back of Deputy Walsh's patrol car as it eases out on to the macadam.

Sam waves to him.

Deputy Thomas speeds east over the mountain with Jared in the rear of the patrol car. He is sick to his stomach from the pot and begins to worry about his mom and how she'll handle this. What will she think when they call her from county jail? And his old man, he'll go ballistic. Jail for God's sake. Will he be fingerprinted and cuffed? Suddenly the patrol car heads over the underpass rather than north up toward the county jail in San Rafael.

The deputy clears his throat. "Now Jared, get this, I don't want to meet you again. You understand? This appears to be your first incident and I'm opting to giving you a talk-to. I don't want to see you in any more trouble. And if I do, we'll throw the book at you. Get it?"

"Yes, sir."

"We decided we would let you and your friend off this time. But this is it. I'm taking you home and we're going to have a little talk with your parents. Your folks probably won't like getting out of bed at two in the morning.

The deputy checks his rearview mirror. He studies the sandy-haired, blue-eyed blonde kid to see if the words have registered.

"I'm not going to jail?" He heaves a sigh of relief. Thinks a moment, then says,"My folks are going to be really pissed when they see a squad car come up the drive. I've never been in this kind of trouble before."

"Well, see this doesn't happen again."

"My mom will probably cry and my old man will be mad as hell. They're having a huge party tomorrow and he's going to hit the roof."

Deputy Thomas pulls into the driveway at 430 Belvedere Way. "Jared, you live in a house like this? How could a kid go wrong living in a place like this? Man, this is a palace!"

Jared just shrugs and looks down at his feet.

As they approach the oak-paneled double door, he overhears his parents' raised voices through the open den window. He looks at Sgt. Thomas. Has he noticed?

His jaw grows taut, his fists clench.

Thomas rings the bell. The noisy arguing continues.

After pausing a few moments, the deputy pounds on the door with his fist this time. Apparently the occupants can't hear the bell or the knocking. Jared shuffles his feet and stares down at the marbled steps.

Thomas hears a soft weepy voice, "This is the last party I'm going to plan. Meeting your exacting standards and the demands of your clients is too much. I don't have fun at my own parties. Lately all we do is entertain for business. When was the last time we just had our friends over? In fact, I don't know whether we have any friends any more, we rarely see them." The woman's voice grows shrill. "I'm so on edge these days, nervous and worried, thinking will the roast be a perfect medium rare? Or will the wine be chilled to your specific temperature level? Will Maria offer the hors d'oeuvres enough times to your wealthiest clients? Will my weight be down far enough? Do I have to go out and buy another high fashion designer dress that is too expensive and too ridiculous looking in order to keep up with the other women at my party? Will my French be absolutely perfect when I speak with Mrs. Duvelle, who, by the way, wants to seduce you."

A male voice cuts in, "Sally, you stop your damned whining. I've just about had enough with you and your ridiculous insinuations. All I want is for you to be perfect and these parties to be perfect; do you understand?"

Jared and the deputy hear a pounding on a table. "Because of these clients and because of Mimi Duvelle's husband, we get to live in this Taj Mahal of a house. These clients pay for our kids to go to that expensive private school. They pay for your elegant lifestyle, so you're going to pay them back. You're going to smile and be gracious. There will be no screw-ups. Got that!"

"Are you threatening me?

"Yes, I'm threatening you."

"I'm not intimidated by you!"

"Maybe this will teach you to do as I say."

There is a sharp smack and a slight cry.

Outside Deputy Thomas glances over at Jared. The kid looks ready to barge through the door. The deputy gently takes Jared's arm to block him. "Hey in there, this is the police."

He pounds again with more force. After a moment of silence, the door opens and a tall red-faced, lean middle-aged man dressed in chinos and a tattersall shirt stares out at them. He is frowning, his shoulders taut, glacial blue eyes glaring. He sizes up the deputy.

"Is everything all right in there, sir?"

"Certainly, officer, everything is fine in here. There's no need for alarm."

Jim frowns, "Jared, what's going on here?"

"Sir, I'm returning your son to you. There's been some trouble."

His father looks at Jared with contempt, "What the hell do you mean by trouble, officer?"

"May we come in, sir, and discuss this matter with you inside?" As they walk down the wide hallway, the deputy proceeds to explain what has occurred. "Your son was over at Muir Beach with his friends tonight. We got a call from our dispatcher. Folks on the hill phoned the police station and made a complaint about a bonfire. They were worried it would set all of Muir Beach ablaze. Also, these young men were smoking marijuana and drinking beer."

"Hey wait a minute, deputy, my son smoke marijuana? I have to correct you on that. It's impossible. Jared is a straight-A student at Marin Academy and on his way to a top Ivy League school. He has never been in trouble before. You're mistaken. I'm sure it was the other guys. Not Jared."

Deputy Thomas looks about furtively for the female he has heard, "Sir, just for the record, could I have your name and the names of all the people residing in this residence?"

"Certainly, I can be cooperative with the law; I'm Jim Boothe, I live here with my wife, Sally Boothe, Jared, my son, and also my daughter, Jennifer. We have live-in help, Maria, our maid."

"Thanks, and Maria's last name?

"Eschovar."

As the deputy jots notes on his notepad, father and son glare menacingly at each other.

"Sir, we need to talk a little more about the situation at the beach, could we please sit down and discuss this?"

Jim signals him to move into the living room. Deputy Thomas follows, unobtrusively scanning for the female figure he has heard.

He continues with his questioning, "I decided not to book him at county jail. He's so young. I told him we'd speak with you and Mrs. Boothe about this situation and try and figure out how not to have it happen again. Is Mrs. Boothe up and about? May I speak with her?"

As they enter the vast well-lit living room, the floor-to-ceiling windows offer a panoramic view of the bay. Off to the east, the Oakland lights are twinkling and then to the south, the vast intensity of the lights in the office buildings in downtown San Francisco sparkle in the dark night and lastly toward the west, the lights flash atop the Golden Gate Bridge.

A slight figure lingering almost behind the soft-flowing drapes at the windows emerges out of the shadows.

The deputy introduces himself. "I'm Deputy Thomas, and you must be Mrs. Boothe. I don't want you to be alarmed Mrs. Boothe, but Jared was in some trouble this evening."

She is incredibly beautiful with what is known as a peaches and cream complexion, sapphire blue eyes, and a radiant halo of closely cropped curly blonde hair. There appears to be a slight reddening over her left check. Her hand is partially covering it.

"Good evening, officer, I see from your badge, you're a sergeant." She smiles at the deputy and gestures for him to have a seat on the plush velvet settee. "Would you like to have a cup of coffee?" she suggests.

The deputy nods. She leaves momentarily, then returns. Those blue eyes never leave the deputy's face as she focuses her total attention upon making him feel welcome. Only then does she move towards Jared and give her son a comforting hug. Grim-faced, Jared returns the hug, and then pats her on the shoulder. He doesn't release her. He moves his arm around her waist protectively.

"Now what seems to be the problem, Sergeant Thomas? My dear Jared couldn't possibly have been in any trouble. I'm sure it's as Mr. Boothe explained to you in the hallway. Jared has never been in this sort of trouble before."

A figure in a blue terrycloth bathrobe appears.

"Deputy Thomas, this is Maria, she runs our household."

Maria places a porcelain cup of coffee with sugar and cream on the table next to the settee within easy reach of the deputy. As she leaves, she glances comfortingly at Jared. The deputy explains the circumstances to the Boothes. While listening to the deputy, Jim is pacing back and forth; his face red with rage. He glares at his son, whose long, lanky physique is also taut with tension. Jared glares back. He's seen the red welt. His fists are clenched. It appears he wants to hit his father.

"To be honest with you, Mr. and Mrs. Boothe, I didn't have the heart to book Jared. He appears to be a good kid, very polite, and too he is so young, just a freshman at Marin Academy, I understand. Our booking sergeant would have put him in the juvenile detention center and that environment hardens kids."

Sally responds, "Oh Deputy Thomas, how discerning of you to recognize Jared as basically a good boy. This is probably just an act of mischief. I am so indebted to you for the course of action you chose to take. She turns and says, "Aren't we grateful to the deputy, Jim?"

"How the hell should I know, Sally? The kid's under your supervision, you're his mother. Frankly, I don't understand my son anymore, officer. He won't toe the line. I'm up to here with his behavior lately." He makes a motion across his neck. "Actually, maybe you should have booked him in the county clink. That might do him some good."

Sally gasps.

Jared stands rigid. He gives his father a contemptuous glare.

Thomas gives Jim a hard look. "To be honest with you, sir, I think I've taken the best course of action possible. You've got what looks to me like a fine son here, despite what's happened this evening."

He frowns at Jim and says. "Jared and I had a chance to have a long talk in the cruiser on the way back from Muir Beach. Now I've made you both aware and am repeating again, your teenage son was drinking beer and I must emphasize, he's under age. He also was smoking marijuana, both of which are misdemeanors. Collectively these infractions could have serious consequences." The deputy takes a deep breath, saying, "If you don't mind sir, I'd like to ask you how much time you spend with Jared, and do you both get along?"

Jim explodes, "Officer, you're prying into our personal affairs. I can get you on invasion of privacy for that question."

"Actually, legally you can't do that, Mr. Boothe, I was simply exploring the reasons for Jared's risky behavior."

"That's none of your business."

The deputy puts his coffee cup down and faces Jim squarely.

Sally intercedes. "Now Sergeant Thomas, Mr. Boothe is rather upset and perhaps overreacting after hearing all of this news. Please forgive him. It's not every day that people of our sort have a deputy come to our door.

You know, we're the kind of people you, yourself, usually never meet."

"Thanks for the apology, Mrs. Boothe. I think it's time for me to move on. We've covered all bases here. But there is something else I'd like to bring up with you, specifically."

"Yes?"

"I'm an officer of the law, ma'am, and responsible for the public safety. I couldn't help noticing when Jared and I stood waiting outside the door we overhead what seemed to me to be a physical altercation."

Jim turns ashen.

"You're mistaken," Sally states firmly.

"Ma'am, what is that red welt over your left check?"

"Oh that," she pauses, "I tripped over the rug in these high heels and fell against the Winthrop highboy in the hall. You know these heels are fashionable, but they are not really practical."

"How often do those heels cause you problems, Mrs. Booth?"

"Occasionally."

"Occasionally?" Deputy Thomas pauses, letting the word hang in the air.

She nods.

The sergeant continues gently, "You know it's interesting, we have a high incidence of women in Marin tripping and falling down stairs because of heels like that. We've seen some heavy duty bruising because of those heels. We discuss it at headquarters a lot. It's kind of interesting though, the bruises many times don't indicate a fall, and the injuries are located mostly on the face, not on the body. We find that rather strange, don't you?"

Jim interrupts, "Well, sergeant we've heard enough of your theories. Thank you for bringing my son home. I'll be sure to speak to him about these transgressions of his tomorrow morning at breakfast." He signals for the deputy to move down the hallway. As they approach the door the sergeant inexplicably shifts his hefty girth and lurches into Jim bumping him into the Winthrop highboy. Jim staggers and falls.

"Oh, sir, I'm so sorry, a faulty heel on my shoes made me trip. So sorry, sir, hope you're okay."

"I'll have your badge for this," says Jim pulling himself upright.

"I don't think so, sir. It was an accident and I apologize. A faulty heel, sir. Any bruises or pain? Any welts on your face?"

Jim glowers.

Since the deputy receives no answer, he moves towards the door, and shakes hands with Jared, who has wisely chosen to stand aside. "Good luck, son," says Thomas. "Anytime you want to come up to my office and shoot the bull, just drop in, you hear. Here's my card."

Jared follows the deputy out the door and says, "Deputy Thomas, thanks for letting me off the hook. I know what we did was wrong. I might drop in sometime to let you know how everything is going."

Thomas looks back at Jim, who is listening at the doorway, "I hope you do that, son."

As the sergeant pulls the cruiser away and eases down the drive, Jared hears the deputy whistling. Could that be the theme from "The Bridge on the River Kwai?" The whistling continues and then fades as the patrol car slowly moves toward Tiburon Boulevard.

Jared begins to smile. Then he begins to hum the refrain. Then he laughs. As he reenters the house and swiftly moves down the hallway towards the kitchen, he sees his folks sitting at the antique pine kitchen table. He immediately strides towards his father, who slowly rises. But then Jared changes his mind, and turns and makes his way up the stairs towards his bedroom.

Jim yells at him, "We'll talk about tonight's nonsense tomorrow morning at breakfast, Jared."

"Yes, sir."

As he reaches the top of the landing, he hesitates and leans over the banister, "Mom, Sergeant Thomas took a real interest in your safety, didn't he?" Jared glares over the railing at his dad.

His mother glances up at him, "Well I suppose he did, dear."

"I don't think he liked what he heard outside the door." Jared stares at his father, saying, "And you know what, Mom? I didn't like it either."

Sally doesn't meet Jared's eyes as she responds, "Oh honey, you know Dad and I have our moments. Don't worry your handsome head about it. It was nothing really. Sergeant Thomas probably misinterpreted what was happening in here." She turns away to rearrange the etched-glass Tiffany hurricane lamps on the sideboard.

"But I haven't misinterpreted it, Mom."

She looks at him sharply and murmurs softly, "Jared, have a good night's sleep, dear. You've been through enough tonight. Get some rest. Don't be troubling yourself about matters that don't concern you." She gives him a quick look of warning.

"If you need me Mom, I'm here."

She opens her mouth, hesitates, and then closes it.

He pauses a few seconds on the landing, still glaring at his dad, then says.

"Good night, Mom."

He heads down the carpeted hallway towards the solace of his bedroom. As he enters he thinks, some day he will visit with Sergeant Thomas, for sure, some day he will. A cool guy, the sergeant, a cool guy.

JJ Vineyards

Jim's Story

Jim Boothe turns left off of St. Helena Highway and pulls up to the latched fence. He swiftly slides his towering frame out of the silver Jaguar and unhitches the sagging gate, then returns to his car, moves it forward a few feet, gets out and re-hitches the gate behind him. As he grudgingly climbs back into his car, he thinks, so much for owning twenty acres of prime vineyard property, every time you enter or leave you have to spend unnecessary time hitching gates.

Easing up the winding hill through the stand of madrone, oak, and red-barked manzanita and approaching the hilltop, he experiences a long, yearned for sense of relief. As he gazes at the sun-dappled vineyards, instead of succumbing to the usual feeling of disgruntlement over the past few years, he is very pleased. The vineyards look really good, damned good. The early spring pruning has paid off. Young tender leaves are beginning to appear on the vines. Soon there will be a hint of an abundance of tiny new grapes tucked beneath. His last two harvests had been disasters. The acidic content of the grapes had been much too high. Maybe there is a real future for JJ Vineyards. Perhaps a few years from now, he'd have enough courage to enter a bottle in the prestigious Orange County Fair. Who knows, he might even place.

At the top of the hill, the sunlight on the mustard blossoms growing between the vines catches his eye. At this time of year, those bright yellow blossoms give all of the Napa Valley a golden hue. It's as if Mother Nature has announced, "Enough of this dreary, rainy season and heavy fog. I'm going to coat the valley in buttery yellow to lift your spirits." The sight warms Jim Boothe's heart. Perhaps it's an omen, now, at last, the vineyard will flourish.

Out of the corner of his eye, he sees a shadow of a figure moving up the ridge. Strange, he assumed Salvador had all the crew working down along the highway smoothing that surface for more planting. He had instructed him to have the workers clear out all the extraneous debris, wanting to utilize every extra inch of land for new plantings.

He spies Annette pruning the vines at the top of the ridge. Her blonde curly hair peeks out over the top of the vines. God, he is lucky to have hired her. She has not only graduated top of her class in viticulture at the University of California-Davis, but she is downright gorgeous. When neighboring vintners visit, they often give Jim an envious glance as they catch a glimpse of her.

Easing the Jaguar in front of the custom-designed garage doors, he smiles at the artistic embellishments. He had at first balked at his wife's hair-brained idea of custom garage doors. But the sense of luxury the wood carvings on the doors exude as visitors approach up the meandering driveway conveys a vision of a prestigious upscale farmhouse right out of Provence. Sally had a famous local woodcarver etch Picasso's bouquet of flowers right into the soft pliable wood. It cost a fortune to have it done, but it was worth it.

"If we're going to measure up to those stuffy well-to-do Easterners who now live in 'the valley,' we have to go for the unique, Jim."

"Well, Sally, this estimate from the woodcarver is sure unique." He continued, "Just this garage door will take half the capital we've assigned to the farmhouse restoration."

"Look at it as a marketing tool," she stated. "You said the next step for the vineyard is marketing the wines. When people drive up for wine-tastings, this will set the tone, signaling it's a prestigious vineyard."

"Isn't there any less expensive way we can use to set this prestigious tone?"

"Trust me, Jim, I know what I'm doing."

"Well you usually do, Sal, but it's going to beat the hell out of our budget."

Now, as he looks at those doors, he has to hand it to her, she does have superb taste.

Getting out of the Jaguar, he moves down the hillside in the direction of Annette. Edging his towering, taut body through the trellises, he hears the distant murmur of the workers' voices over by the highway. They're busy clearing rocks and pebbles below the ridge out of view. Is the entire valley made of rock? He had been told the early glaciers moved through, scraping up the valley floor and then receded, dropping huge boulders and stones in its wake. Thanks to the movement of the glacier ten thousand years ago, he is spending a fortune on stone removal.

Even though he's anxious to see Annette and get her take on the status of the grapes, he pauses to check the recent growth of the vines. The young leaves are beginning to drape over the trellis wiring. They have that early tinge of asparagus green. Richer shades will emerge later in the summer as crush draws closer. As he begins to adjust a few of the tendrils that have fallen off the trellis, he hears a sharp scream and scuffling a few feet away. He looks up.

My God, Juan Yolandez has Annette down on the ground with pruners at her neck. He has his hand between her legs. He's trying to yank down her shorts. Jim moves swiftly. Annette appears to be shoving to get out from under Juan, but she's impeded by the pruners in her face. Her eyes are wild with rage. She's scratching at him, attempting to push him off, but his weight is pinning her down.

As Jim reaches them, he yells, "Son of a bitch, get off her." He lurches towards Juan, knocking the pruners aside. They tumble down the hill and crash into the next tier of adjoining vines. "You dirty spic, what the hell are you doing?" Jim shouts.

Juan appears seemingly contrite as he quickly raises himself off the ground, "Sorry, Señor Boothe." Then he flashes a lurid grin at Annette.

"You get off my property. You get your goddamn ass out of here. And don't come back. Do you hear? I'll see you never work in this valley again."

Juan looks at him menacingly. He looks down at the pruning shears.

"Not my fault, Señor. She motioned to me."

Annette gasps.

Jim wants to kill him. He smacks him across the face with his fist. The force knocks Juan off his feet. Jim towers over him with fists clenched. It is all he can do to contain himself. He knows if he smashes him to smithereens it will bring notoriety to the valley. The neighboring vintners will be outraged believing Jim should have handled this quietly. He checks himself. *I'll destroy this guy later, my way.*

As Juan rises, Jim warns, "Go! Right now or I'll call the sheriff."

They hear Salvador approaching. Jim's crew supervisor has been drawn by the noise. When Juan sees Salvador hurrying up the hill, he scurries swiftly back down the ridge toward the highway.

"What's the trouble, Señor?" asks Salvador.

"I pay you to supervise this farm crew. Juan had Annette down on the ground. I never want to see him on my place again, do you understand? You keep a better eye out. You're to see these guys keep out of trouble."

"Si, Señor. I'm sorry, but I can't be everywhere at once."

"Don't give me that stuff; that's your job! You should have noticed he was missing from the crew. I'll call down to the Farm Bureau and he'll be out of the valley tonight. I don't care if he has six kids to support, he's finished."

Salvador shrugs.

Disgusted, Jim waves him off and turns toward Annette, "Come on, Annette. Let's see to those bruises. Are there any cuts or scrapes?"

Annette rests against a pile of rocks, quietly sobbing.

"No, he didn't really hurt me, I'm just shaken up a bit," she gasps. "He took me completely by surprise. I sensed he was hovering around, but never thought he'd try something like this." She tries to catch her breath. "I was leaning over inspecting the root system of a vine when he jumped me."

"Well, I'm sure glad I got here when I did. Where the hell is Jerry? He's supposed to be here on the grounds."

"He's down in St. Helena at the lab talking to the technicians about last year's crop of grapes. He's trying to learn how to make a closer call on the acidic content at harvest this year."

"Are you sure you're all right?"

She nods, but struggles to maintain her composure. Her gasps for breath seem to be easing a bit.

He helps her up the slate steps to the back of the farmhouse and as they enter the kitchen, he checks out the pantry for the First Aid kit. He swabs Annette's elbow and left shin where there are scrapes. She is weeping softly now. He wants to put his arms around her and comfort her. He tries to avoid staring at the curve of her shin. He shifts a bit away.

This is the perfect time to warn her. He's been meaning to do this for some time. But how is he going to tell his knowledgeable viticulturist she has a body that turns men on? How is he going to approach the subject of her wearing no bra under her Izod tee shirts, and advise her to wear jeans instead of shorts? Besides, why the hell did he have to do that anyway?

But he's seen the workers watching her. And he knows today's incident was just waiting to happen. He'd call

Len Brown down at the California Farm Service Bureau and report what had occurred. Len will quietly take care of this. Juan will be sent away, never to earn a dime in the valley again.

Jim finishes the bandaging and pulls away as he studies her carefully. He feels embarrassed, but knows this is the appropriate time to bring up the wardrobe problem. In the back of his head he's wondering how he can best approach the subject. "You still seem to be shaken. Take the afternoon off. This has been quite a shock for you. It must have taken a lot out of you."

"I'll be okay. I'm just glad you got here when you did." She is still noticeably shaking. "It could have been much worse. I couldn't scream for help, he had the pruners right there in my face." She takes a deep breath, "Yes, I'm a little bit shaky, but in a few days, I'll be over it." She smiles ruefully, saying, "Remember I'm a sturdy character, I come from French peasant stock."

He laughs. "Okay, but we've got to learn from this experience. I'm trying to figure out how to prevent this from happening again. I'm responsible for you, you know. I promised your father I'd watch over you. I feel badly about what has happened on my property. He smiles down at her and then says, "You know you are a good-looking young woman. I know it sounds foolish, but do you think there is something you could do to make yourself less attractive?" He looks down at the tiled-floor and then suggests awkwardly, "Maybe wear jeans instead of shorts? It's early spring and it isn't that hot out yet."

He stares into her tear-filled blue eyes, which never

fail to distract him. Now he's almost experiencing those same licentious thoughts Juan had. How could he explain the male testosterone level to her?

She surprises him by drawing herself bolt upright. "I suppose so, but why do I have to change my behavior? They should change theirs. Why can't you speak to them?"

"Oh, I will; don't get me wrong. I'll instruct Salvador to warn them if anything else occurs they're not only off this place, but out of the valley. They've probably already heard what Juan has done. And he's toast because of it. But you've got to do your part too. Just try the jeans!"

She grins, "Okay, Jim, I'll do what you ask. I might even put on a shroud."

He laughs and says, "Well you don't have to go that far." He can't bring himself to mention wearing a bra. His eyes graze across the Izod tee-shirt. He can see her breasts so clearly defined.

They sit silently at the old pine kitchen table, each coming to terms with their own thoughts. Jim reflects on Annette's youthful lushness. She's curvaceous in the right places, but spare too, from her heavy work in the vineyards. He had been aroused before when looking at her, but sublimated it in protectiveness towards her. She is young. She had been in the states now for almost six years. Her family is back in France. She is still making her way in a new country and has only a few friends up here in Napa.

Gazing out the window and viewing the serpentine trellises, covering the hilltop and edging toward the valley floor, he reminisces about how Annette and Jerry arrived at JJ Vineyards. His new viticulturist had received her Bachelor of Science at UC Davis and came highly recommended by the department head. Jerry Torello, of the Mondavi family, accepted his offer to become manager of the vineyard. The two were considered the best of the bunch in Napa for their expertise in raising premiere grapes. Both Jerry and Annette had come from families that went back three generations in the wine making industry, so they grew up with grape stains etched into their hands. Jerry's forbearers started a vineyard here in Napa right before Prohibition. And Annette's family produced record breaking crops of burgundy in the Loire Valley.

One dreary rain-soaked afternoon in late November after experiencing another disastrous harvest, Jim had interviewed and made the decision to hire both of them. In celebration, he decanted a bottle of 1970 private reserve. Under the influence of those two bottles of his Sauvignon Blanc, a friendly get-acquainted conversation ensued. The wine helped reduce the tension of the new employee-employer relationship. Jim vented his frustration over the failure of his past harvests. Jerry and Annette opened up and shared what it was like to grow up on grape farms and their years of sitting at the family table as youngsters, hearing passionate family arguments about when to prune, what to do about irrigation problems, and of course most importantly, when to crush. This had prepared both Jerry and Annette for their present vocations here in "the valley."

Annette opened up and relaxed by the wine, giggled, "I remember the tension in my family was so fierce right before harvest. My old rickety grandmere chased my grandpere around the kitchen table with a butcher knife meant for chopping *coq au vin* when she felt the harvest had been delayed too long."

Jerry shrugged and said, "Okay, I've got a better one." He grinned. "That's nothing! Every evening after family dinners, my three brothers and I would have a stand-off out in the vineyards. We'd beat the you-know-what out of each other to release the nervous tension of waiting out the time to crush. When crush finally came we would forget everything. We'd work like hell to get those grapes out of the fields and in to any available gondola."

As Jim listened to Annette and Jerry, his thoughts shifted to the old tradition of family dinners within his own household. What had happened to his own family? Why the hell didn't they ever eat together any more? He remembered the dinners of his childhood, just like the family dinners Annette and Jerry were talking about. Boy, when the Larkspur Firehouse whistle went off at five o'clock in the evening, he and his friends had to stop playing and head for home. They would be in big trouble if they weren't sitting at the dinner table with hands washed and hair combed. All the members of his family, his stern pop, and his brother and three sisters had to show up no matter what was going on. There was no fooling at the table. It was "yes sir" and "no sir" to his pop. Anyone who misbehaved was whacked in the head.

When had his present family dinners disappeared? Years ago, Sally would prepare wonderful home cooked meals when Jared and Jen were little. He remembered the macaroni and cheese she served when they were starting out. Jeez, he loved that macaroni and cheddar cheese. She'd gotten the recipe from his mom. But now, these days, she seemed to have to brace herself to face any of them during their infrequent evening meals.

A few months ago, she'd tried to pull it all back together and started seeing a psychiatrist. That crazy shrink, Dr. Blinder. She had even begun to serve the macaroni and cheese again.

"Dinner time, everybody." She waited a few moments, then called out again.

Jen eventually appeared, "Mom, that looks so good, but you know I'm dieting to keep my weight down for swim."

"Just try it, Jen, dear."

"I'm going upstairs and nibble on these carrot sticks."

Sally shrugged.

Jared appeared at the door, "Hey, awesome, Mom, I'll take a bowl of the stuff up to my room and work on my computer."

Admittedly, Jim remembered the many evenings he really hadn't helped. He'd arrive home at nine o'clock.

Sally gave up after a few months. Now, for God's sake, she calls the Tiburon Caterer and orders prepared dishes, never touching a frying pan herself. Whenever, he and the kids come home, they find their individual meals in the warming tray on the sideboard.

Without the family meals, he never sees the kids. They all arrive at different times. They both eat as quickly as possible and disappear upstairs to their rooms. Jared to his computer, and Jen to that damn treadmill.

When he does arrive in time for dinner, he notices as

Jen approaches the sideboard and sees the catered prepared meal, she sniffs with disdain and heads for the frig for a bowl of her "veggies," as she calls them. He had attempted to get home when she did and engage her in conversation. But it didn't work. After a few words, it was as if she was driven to get upstairs and on to that machine. Strangely though, she was not only disappearing on him, she was disappearing, period. She appeared lost in her clothes. They hung on her. The "grunge" look she called it. My God, he works eighteen-hour days to earn a living to provide them with enough money to live like kings and queens, and here's his kid walking around looking like a starving pauper, turning up her nose at the best catered meals one could have.

And Jared. He and that kid have passed the point of no return. Jared seemed downright angry with him all the time. He couldn't get to the bottom of it. He had such hopes for his son. He tried to sign him up for tennis lessons at the club, so they could play tennis together. He had a Saturday morning foursome every week and he hoped Jared would develop his tennis enough so they could meet right after the foursome. He wanted to show off his son. But then Jared goes and pulls the stunt of the season and embarrasses him in front of his friends.

* * * * *

Yesterday, while standing on the deck of the Tiburon Ferry in the late afternoon sunshine, Jim's commuting buddy, Pete, cautioned Jim not to worry. Gulping down his double martini Pete explained, "Look, Jimbo! You've got to understand our male teenage offspring. They are moving into manhood and testing us all the way. Bouncing against us like trout moving upstream."

"You've got that right. But why do they have to make such asses out of us? I mean, the other day at the tennis club it was as if Jared intentionally wanted to humiliate me.

"Hey, it's their way. You've got to learn to live with it. Ignore it. By the way, do you know, they are meeting for weekly rituals of bonfires over at Muir Beach on Friday nights? Be glad they're on the other side of Marin away from us for a few hours. Crazy kids."

Jim knew only too well where Jared was on Friday evenings. He stared off at the seals playing on the buoys. What a pleasure it was to travel by ferry. It was so relaxing. He really enjoyed the picturesque scenery surrounding the San Francisco Bay. But because the trip took so long, he only permitted himself this treat once a week. He wished he could allow himself time to do it more often. But now he was trying to get home by car as quickly as possible to be with the family.

Last night he had made a special effort to arrive early hoping to be with them. There was Sally sitting out on the deck watching the sun set beyond the Golden Gate. She was lost in the moment with her usual glass of wine. It stood there half full or should he say half empty.

"Hi Sal, how are you doing?" He leaned over and his lips brushed her cheek. She withdrew just a bit out of his reach. It was an imperceptible gesture to others, but never to him.

She did not look up at him, "Just fine, how was your day?"

Was she slurring?

He studied her, then remarked, "Sure glad it's Friday. Where are the kids?"

"Jen had to go to swim practice and Jared took off for Muir Beach for a barbeque." She shifted around to view the sunset.

Even though Sal appeared testy, and this maybe wasn't the time, he decided to bring up the subject they were never able to discuss. He considered for a moment. Was it because they were too scared to approach the unspoken? Was it because they wanted to avoid an argument? Nevertheless, he began, "How many swim meets does Jennifer have to go to? Have you noticed she seems to literally be swimming her fanny off lately?" He sat down close to Sally, wanting to draw her in. "It worries me. Have you seen her? She's disappearing on us. She's getting smaller and smaller."

Sally sloughed it off, "It's okay, don't worry. It's a healthy activity. Don't concern yourself with it"

He shook his head, shrugged, gave up and went inside to the sideboard to pour himself some of the vineyard's sauvignon blanc private reserve. Christ, Sally never drank it. She said it is too acidic. She couldn't even bring herself to drink his wine, much less have sex with him.

When he returned to the deck the sun was just peaking over the ridges of Sausalito and the lights of that upscale Mediterranean-like community were twinkling on. They sat silently watching the sun disappear. Jim luxuriated in this picture perfect view. He'd earned this. The tension in his neck seemed to vanish and he felt his shoulders lowering to their natural position.

Sally was facing west caught in the dimming shadows.

She was still quite beautiful with those classical, patrician looks that come from good breeding. His blue-eyed, blonde-haired Waspian wife, in spite of her drinking, still appeared to be fit and trim. And she carried herself with such poise. She charmed his clients. They adored her. He noticed her eyes were tearing. She glanced at him and ruefully made a gallant effort to smile as she brushed aside the tears.

He suddenly became uncomfortable with this tearful display of emotion. He'd never been comfortable with female tears. Inexplicably, his heart suddenly hardened. He chose to ignore her attempts at composure.

"So Jared's over at Muir Beach with his buddies? When I was a kid we stayed in the neighborhood. I guess he prefers to be elsewhere rather than at home. You know that kid went out of his way to embarrass me at the tennis club last Saturday? Can you beat that?"

Sally shrugged her shoulders and stared at him.

"Here I make an attempt to be with him more and set up a match for us. And what does he do? He shows up at the club looking like Jerry Garcia dressed in a black tee shirt and black jeans. He knows the club has a dress code of tennis whites." He looked directly at her, "For Christ sake Sal, I'm trying to connect with him and here he goes and does a fool thing like that. Thank God, nobody important was there."

She glared at him. She looked as if she wanted to hit him. What's come over her? She's never looked at me like that before. But he taunted, "They're your kids, Sal. You've got to shape up, you're not doing your job by them."

Her arm swung wide and shattered her Baccarat glass.

Shards of crystal slithered across the teak table. She looked down at the broken serrated stem. For a few moments she sat gazing at the stem and then a strange look appeared on her face. Was she considering using it as a weapon? She shifted her weight, facing him directly.

He swiftly retreated into the dining room to get out of range and poured himself another glass of wine from the bottle on the sideboard. What the heck is going on with her? She looked maniacal out there.

The outside lights on the deck and adjoining terrace needed to be turned on. Why wasn't there some semblance of order in this household? He made his way through the levels of the house switching off upper bedroom lights and turning on the hallway and entrance lights. He checked the stove to make sure the burners were off. Good, everything was in order. Or was it? Why had Sally lost it and pulled that crazy stunt?

He stood just inside of the doorway of the deck to check her out. She appeared to be calm now, watching the sun finally set beyond the Golden Gate Bridge. He wondered if he should report this episode to her psychiatrist. After all, she appeared violent. He did decide to set up an appointment with Dr. Blinder The doctor had told him Sally was trying to work out her problems and reduce her tension and anger. My God, why was she experiencing tension? She was living in this eight million dollar mansion in one of the most beautiful places in the world. She had all her material needs met and any staff she wanted to help her maintain the household. He asked the good doctor for an explanation as to what was troubling her and why she was so tense.

"Mr. Boothe, what do you think is troubling Sally?"

"I don't know, I'm asking you. Maybe she has too much time on her hands. To the good, she seems to have cut back on her drinking somewhat, since she's been seeing you. She's really keeping it under control. I'm grateful for that. We're having a big shindig next Friday and I don't want any trouble, if you know what I mean."

"Mr. Boothe, what do you think is troubling Sally?"

My God, this guy is an ass. He's already asked me that. I've showed him my appreciation, what does he want? He's not saying anything, he just keeps staring at me from under those bushy eyebrows.

"Mr. Boothe?"

"Yes."

"Mr. Boothe?"

Is this guy nuts? This is costing $200 an hour. For interrogation?

"Mr. Boothe, Jim, it might be appropriate for us, for you and me to continue to meet privately for a few sessions. We could concentrate on what might be causing Sally's problems? I think a few discussions with you might help Sally."

"Doc, listen, what would I have to do with Sally's problems? You've got to meet with Sally to settle her problems with her. I'm just fine. Now I know in some marriages, its cause and effect. But not with me. Yep, I'm just fine. It's her thought processes that you need to adjust. Get my drift?"

"Then why are you here, Jim, discussing Sally, if everything is fine? It's your household too you know, you sound as if you have concerns."

That damnable clock keeps ticking and ticking. The doctor is still trying to stare me down. What's the guy up to? He's charging me $200 an hour for a staring contest? Maybe Sally should see someone else.

* * * * *

Now as Jim sits in the kitchen with Annette, he gazes out at the tight orderly tiers of vines. That's the way he wants his life to be, orderly. He tries not to think of last night. He has no idea what had come over Sally. She had never behaved that way before. She was almost feral in her actions. He knew she wanted to take a swipe at him. In fact, he is the one who usually took the swipes. I guess this is called "role reversal," a la Dr. Blinder. She hadn't even come upstairs. She'd stayed out on the deck all night sipping wine. He heard her easing into the other side of the bed around five o'clock. He left for Napa about an hour later without waking her.

Pondering it all on the drive north, he wondered if he should have made plans with her to join him this morning. The drive up to Napa together could have given them a chance to be alone. He remembered whenever Sally came up to the vineyard, which was infrequently, she enjoyed it. She would take long hikes across the valley floor and over to the long, winding Silverado Trail. She seemed hell-bent on physically tiring herself out, just like Jennifer. Sally liked being with Annette and practiced speaking French with her. She had been a French major at Wellesley. They would sit out by the pool together in the late afternoon sun and converse, giggling over Sally's attempts to make sense. Of course there would be the usual bottle of wine between them.

Mixed Signals

* * * * *

As he gazes out the vast picture window at the views across the valley floor, he studies Annette, musing about how she might regard him. He imagines she views him as a father-employer figure. He wonders whether he might be attractive to her. There have been no signals on her part. He knows he's attractive to other women. They seem to like his towering height and compact figure and his blue-eyed, sandy haired Waspian looks seem to pass muster.

Suddenly Annette rises, interrupting his thoughts, "I'd better get back outside, Jim, and complete the inspection of the root system."

He attempts to delay her by remaining seated and he takes a chance, asking, "Are you sure you're okay, do you want to take the afternoon off? Let me take you to lunch down in St. Helena?"

There is a small frown and then her gaze softens.

"No, Jim. No lunch. I'd better get right back out and be alone by myself in the vineyards. If I delay, I'll become permanently afraid and not want to work there again." She pauses and seems to be collecting her thoughts, murmuring, "Perhaps some other afternoon." She smiles.

He nods mutely. Hey, that might be an opening. Maybe he has hit pay dirt after all. As they leave the kitchen, descending the slate steps, Jerry drives up in the Tucker pickup.

"Where the hell have you been, Jer?"

"Down in town, why?"

Annette moves off toward the vineyard, and Jim gives

Jerry the lowdown.

"I'm not surprised, Jim, she's some piece. I warned you about having a woman out in the vineyards, anyway. Especially her. Her good looks are trouble!"

Jim kicks at a large piece of gravel in the drive, saying, "Now you listen to me, I don't want to hear that Italian macho crap. Your job is to keep an eye on this place."

"Why the hell are you taking it out on me?"

"Well, you should have been here. When I think of what could have happened if I hadn't come along, I blow. Just keep a closer eye out, okay? I spoke to Salvador, too. I want you to call the California Farm Bureau and report what has happened. See that Juan's finished in the valley. And you warn the rest of the crew. We don't want this happening again." He moves toward his car, "I've got to leave now, we're having a big shindig down home this evening. An important client is coming. Hopefully he will provide me with another mil' to sink into this place. My God, Jerry, I've already spent tons of money on this farm. These vineyards just soak up every cent I've got."

Jerry just nods and accompanies him to the car.

As Jim eases down the hill in the Jaguar, he sees Annette and waves. He watches out of his rear-view mirror as she leans over to check out a vine. Those shapely legs are spread apart as she bends over to tie up a loose tendril. My God, no wonder Juan went for her. He wonders whether he should make a move. She certainly gave him permission to try for a future invitation for lunch. Hell no, that's unthinkable. If I had an affair, that would be the end for Sally. She'd file for divorce. I can't take that risk. I would be throwing too much away. There's a lot of wealth we've accumulated together over the years. And there's the kids. I just can't jeopardize that.

His thoughts turn towards Marin as he eases out on to Route 29. Speeding south, he notices his neck is throbbing. His shoulders are scrunched up into his neck vertebrae. Recently every time he approaches home his body signals his frustration. The anger he feels for Sally and the kids builds. Jeez, we have every advantage, why are we all so messed up? Right now, the angry feelings are replacing his contentment with the vineyard and his euphoria over his recent conversation with Annette. He momentarily considers the idea of shucking it all in Marin and moving up to "the valley." It would be a new start. All is going so well up here. The success of the vineyard has given him such a lift. Those new tender vines are bringing a renewed abundance to his life. As he moves through the cow pastures of Sonoma, he yearns to brake and turn around. The closer he draws to Marin the more frustrated he becomes. He wonders, am I'm going in the wrong direction?

Suddenly, he sees a familiar figure up ahead. Could it be Juan making his way out of the valley? The figure is trudging along at the edge of the road. Jim checks his rear-view mirror and then looks ahead. No one else is on the road. He picks up speed rounding the sharp bend. Juan looks up and appears to recognize the car. He begins to take flight when he sees it heading directly for him. He races off the edge of the road tripping into a cement culvert. Jim checks it out as he speeds by. Juan's figure is inert in the ditch, not moving.

Good, thinks Jim. That'll show him.

The throbbing in his neck has ceased. His shoulders are relaxed. It's as if his menacing of Juan has cured his frustration. As he speeds along, he decides to pull his best vintage out of the wine cellar for tomorrow night's party. This shindig should be a celebration. He feels powerful, masterful, able to handle any situation. Why not celebrate?

Douglas County, Colorado

Use of Force

Policy Manual: *Procedures for De-escalation of Use of Force*—Members will use the least amount of force to stop the action of a violator and reduce the amount of force applied as the threat is neutralized or the violator becomes compliant.

What if what Nina says is true? Is it so improbable? I am curious as to why she is confiding all of this to me. We are standing in the parking lot in the late afternoon sun and after listening a bit, my eyes are suddenly drawn to the two huge, white vans belonging to the sheriff and the under-sheriff. Since I know what they contain, their presence is inordinately ominous. Their color of white is deceptively bland to outsiders, suggesting a benign appearance. Black would better suit their true purpose. In structure they are similar to GMC delivery vans. The windows are darkly tinted, so anyone inside is hidden from view. Their huge size and tonnage adds to their menacing appearance. As to their purpose, they seemingly present an innocent image, suggesting they might be used for hauling goods or transporting a number of passengers. All of the members of the Douglas County Sheriffs' Office are fully aware that inside away from view are well-equipped panels and state-of-the-art surveillance equipment with high power weaponry shackled to the roof of the interior.

As Nina continues, I wonder if anyone is sitting inside the vans. Are we being watched? My attention returns to concentrate upon what she is sharing. Nina has reached the rank of sergeant with the Douglas County Sheriff's Office and is intent upon relating what has recently happened this weekend. She is an insider. I don't seem to be catching on to why she is so frazzled. As she continues, my attention is again drawn elsewhere. I notice the last of the Command Staff pulling out of their assigned parking slots into the busy commute traffic. The weekend weather is supposed to be promising. All of us are looking forward to a few balmy days, since we have endured an unusually long, cold winter. Today's temperatures seem to be almost Mediterranean. I glance in the direction of the Rockies. Vestiges of snow still remain on the summit and vertical tiers of ice run down the roughly hewn crevices. I shiver a bit as I catch a glimpse of slivers of the lingering snow sparkling in the sunlight.

Nina's flashing, black, heavily mascared eyes stare at me intently, "Are you aware of what's been happening in the office lately? Have you heard about Deputy Williams?"

"That name is vaguely familiar. Should I know him? Has he been on the tapes you've given me to transcribe?"

She shakes her head, "No, this doesn't have anything to do with tape transcription. Deputy Williams marched in the St. Patrick's Day parade this past weekend. It was the kick-off for the under-sheriff's political campaign for sheriff."

"Well, you know," I smile wryly, "I'm the last to be aware of political matters in the office. I'm one of those who apparently don't matter; insiders share very little with me. But keep going, you know I crave hearing office gossip."

"Deputy Williams made a huge blunder. He marched behind Bowen's truck in the parade. Can you believe that?"

I gasp, "Do you mean he placed himself behind the other candidate's truck, and signified he's backing someone other than the under-sheriff? My gosh, I can't believe he'd take that risk and jeopardize his position in the office."

"He did, and now he's suffering the consequences. The under-sheriff caught up with him after the parade and asked him if he was supporting Bowen.

Williams said, "It's a free country. I can be for any political candidate I want."

"Oh, my gosh."

"Do you know what is happening to Williams because of this?"

"No, as I said before, I'm the last to know."

"This past Monday after the weekend parade he was transferred from Patrol back to Detentions."

"Back to the jail? Nina, I can't believe the under-sheriff would go that far."

"It happened. He's being punished."

"Oh, the poor guy and now he's back as an inmate guard? That's cruel. As I remember he's served his time in the jail for so many years. He's only been on Patrol assignment for six months."

I thought about all of the young deputies who love Patrol. They each have a flashy squad car and dash around town with egos running amuck. Patrol is a coveted, heavily sought after position. On the other hand Detentions with its regimen of guarding unruly inmates day after day is becoming increasingly stressful. The overcrowding in each Mod makes it extremely dangerous. Walking into a cell block filled with one hundred and forty inmates takes an inordinate amount of courage.

Nina continues, "I'm serious. They reassigned him back to Detentions the Monday after he appeared in the parade. It's Williams' own fault. He drew attention to himself. He is publicly showing the entire community whom he supports. It was stupid. Of course the under-sheriff was bent out of shape."

I shake my head, "How can you say it was the deputy's fault? You shouldn't suffer a demotion because of your political choices. How can staff get away with that? And from my perspective as a paralegal in the Legal Advisor's Office I know they can't do that and comply with employment policy. Our office should jump on this in an instant. I wonder why Jim hasn't said anything to me or given me a research assignment on it?"

Nina shakes her finger at me and says, "Now look, you know as well as I, your boss Jim is in close alliance with the under-sheriff. He wouldn't question it. The under-sheriff ordered Williams transferred and what makes you think they're worried about employment policies? Hey, they do whatever they like."

Suddenly, the sheriff and under-sheriff emerge and stride toward their vans. They look in our direction and wave. We obediently wave back.

In spite of the early spring warmth, I again shiver slightly and pull my hand-knit Shetland cardigan closer about my shoulders.

"Nina, please be careful. Don't get involved in this." Somehow, I realize these warnings will fall on deaf ears.

Suddenly we both become aware the VIP vans have not yet left their individual slots. They linger. Are we being watched?

"They haven't pulled out."

"I know. Strange isn't it."

I look apprehensively at my friend and whisper, "We'd better leave."

As I exit the lot and head home, I look in my rearview mirror to see if either of the vans has moved. Sure enough, they've disappeared. Apparently they pulled out right after us. I mull over Nina's story. It seems preposterous. Yes, our organization is in the initial phases of a political campaign for the position of sheriff. Rigid lines have been drawn through the ranks as far as who is supporting whom. Nina, who is very much aligned with and in love with big, burly Sergeant Dave Green, is in the center of the maelstrom. Dave is presently serving as president of the Fraternal Order of Police and the under-sheriff is not pleased with him. He hasn't delivered the potential votes. The FOP which, in the past elections would traditionally back the under-sheriff in his bid for the position of sheriff, is not cooperating. This is causing deep rancor on the under-sheriff's part against those who are opposing him. He is demanding total loyalty from all of staff. Everyone is aware that harsh punishment will be meted out if they deviate from this policy.

The under-sheriff, Bob Hughes, with his sandy-haired, blue-eyed wholesome persona, is young and unseasoned. He's moved up the ladder too fast. The present sheriff took a liking to him and rashly appointed him to serve as under-sheriff, and in the process skipped over an entire tier of older professionals waiting to move up through the ranks. No wonder there is a festering resentment against him.

In retrospect, as for myself, too late in the game did I learn how all of this was going to impact me. My innocent friendship with Nina had unknowingly placed me in jeopardy. A few months ago, the under-sheriff had seen us dining together. This had signaled my coup de grace. She had made arrangements for us to sit two tables away from him. I had been unaware of the gravity of this decision. I thought we would simply be viewed as two gal pals having lunch together. I was not street smart enough to realize that the sheriff could have construed my appearance at the luncheon as a sign that I had become a member of the opposition. In my naiveté I was totally unaware of how he might perceive our innocent tete-de-tete.

Since taking my position at the Douglas County Sheriff's Office, Nina and I have become close friends. Although outwardly this might appear a bit unusual as we both have very little in common. I am considered *less than* as a civilian. "Sworn" personnel are the chosen ones. Civilians are appreciated, but have little power. Few close associations exist between "sworn" and "civies." I am a senior paralegal to the legal advisor to the sheriff. I take pride in my position and like my work. I am constantly challenged by the research I have to do. Issues arise, such as the inmates demanding they want chunky peanut butter rather than creamy. I am the one who researches cases for precedents in order to provide information for the organization's response. To many members of Command Staff, the Legal Advisor's Office is considered a non-essential, a frill. The older seasoned commanders want money for salaries to go to Patrol or Detentions, but with the burgeoning number of lawsuits against the sheriff's office, they are becoming aware of the growing need for on-site legal representation.

Besides the difference in rank, there is a disparity in Nina's and my age. She is in her late thirties and moving up through the ranks. I hope to retire shortly. But what solidified our relationship from acquaintance to best buddies was my compassionate attitude towards her during a very stressful time. Since then she has been a very grateful friend.

Looking back upon that period, I remember how anxious she was. She had had to respond to intense questioning during a deposition from opposing counsel, not easy under most circumstances. The sheriff's office was being sued. The case involved an inmate death and Nina had been the Officer in Charge the night the death occurred. In that capacity, she had made a decision and unfortunately the events that followed were tragic. The inmate had been behaving erratically, wandering about the Mod. All other inmates were in their respective cells. He had been ordered to return to his cell by several deputies. But defiantly he stood on the third floor tier peering over the railing talking to imaginary voices. The deputies began to wonder if he would jump. They reported their concerns to Nina. For his own safety, she ordered him strapped to "the board."

When I first viewed the restraining board, I was horrified and even considered resigning. How could anyone treat human beings like that? But after being counseled it was a necessity, I learned to live with its use. The restraining board is approximately nine feet in length and six feet wide and inmates are strapped face down and secured with leather straps. For even a sane person, it could be very frightening to be restricted in such a manner. Of course, most inmates become very agitated when placed upon it. Their blood pressure and heart rate skyrocket.

In this instance the inmate died of a heart attack. A suit had been instituted against the sheriff's office by the inmate's family and the ACLU.

As I prepared Nina for the depositions, she said, "I had to do what I had to do for his safety and the safety of the deputies."

"Of course you did," I assured her.

"He was hallucinating, talking to voices. I thought he was going to fall off the tier."

I nodded in agreement, "He could have. We all know he shouldn't have been in the jail in the first place. He should have been down in the mental health unit in Pueblo, but since they had no room for him, our jail had to house him." I shook my head, "It's even more ironic to know Pueblo called the next day and said they finally had room for him. As we all know, until a system is set up to put mentally ill inmates in mental health facilities, we have to do our best. And you did the best you could under the circumstances."

"The system stinks and I have to pay for it."

"Yes, you're under the gun with having to respond in this court case, but remember Internal Affairs and Command Staff backed you up one hundred percent. So you know they are totally behind you." With that she hugged me. I had never been hugged by anyone in the Douglas County Sheriff's Office before.

Since then we have become very close, enjoying sushi lunches together, visiting back and forth from office to office sharing office gossip. I feel less like an outsider, thanks to her. I am proud to be her friend; it makes me feel more accepted by the other deputies. It gives me a sense of "belonging" in what appears to me to be a very strange culture. She has achieved a lot. Being a Latino woman in law enforcement is a real coup, especially reaching the rank of sergeant and now being considered for promotion to lieutenant.

As for me, I have grown to depend upon her. When anything comes up that is difficult for me to understand, she interprets this inscrutable world of law enforcement. It is a military environment. Orders are given and obeyed whether they make sense to me or not. Sometimes unbeknownst to all except Nina, I secretly balk when ordered to perform a task I deem totally illogical.

I try to reason with Nina, "But that's crazy for them to do that."

"Yes, but they're doing it," she said, her eyes flashing.

"It doesn't make sense."

"Anne, you have got to learn to play their game."

My days are easier when I follow her advice and think the way she does. Now this afternoon, I am working on tapes she has assigned to me. Transcribing the tapes of the interviews from Internal Affairs is part of my job and I learn an enormous amount about what actually goes on within the organization.

This particular tape is a public relations nightmare waiting to happen. While off duty, one of our young deputies smacked up his patrol car on a curve after he had been drinking late one evening. He had given the Castle Rock Police a hard time when they picked him up and took him down for testing for DUI. He even tried to bribe them. Smart kid. The sheriff, who is overly concerned with appearances, will be furious. There has always been a rivalry between the CRPD and the sheriff's office. This incident will embarrass the sheriff if the local newspaper gets wind of it. I can see the headlines. "Sheriff Unable to Control His Own Deputies." Internal Affairs is investigating, as it does in any case where there is a possibility of wrong doing on the part of staff. The poor kid's head will probably roll when the Findings of Facts reach the sheriff's desk.

I am still working on the tape when Nina pokes her head in my office. "How are you doing with that tape?"

"It's almost done. I wish he hadn't given the CRPD such a hard time after they picked him up for DUI testing." With a certain remorse I thought, when would I stop advocating for the underdog? It has always gotten me in a pile of trouble.

Nina warns, "He knows he's in for it. I'll write up my report and send it up through the chain of command on Monday. He clearly placed himself in jeopardy. By the way, have you heard the latest?"

"What do you mean the latest? Remember, I'm the last

to know being a civilian and a dithering old one at that."

She grins at me and then furtively glances at the doorway of my office as though she half expects someone to come in and catch us talking. She appears apprehensive. This is not Nina.

"Are you ready to leave? I'm on my way out and I want to talk to you in the parking lot."

I turn off the computer, grab my purse and lock the door of my narrow, heavily-strewn legal-papered office. Why, I wonder, in law enforcement when someone has something serious to share do they always leave their offices and discuss it in bars or parking lots? The need to assure themselves they won't be overheard is really paranoid. Initially, I found this behavior amusing. Those who are accustomed to planting bugs become unduly stressed about anything they share with each other of a serious nature. I remember one occasion when the sheriff and Jim, my boss, drove way up to one of the local high schools and sat in the bleachers watching the football team practice. It seemed incongruous to picture them, up at the top of the stadium in their warm wool business suits with the blazing hot September sun beating down upon them, sharing whatever clandestine information they deemed to be confidential. When they returned, Jim told me he and the sheriff had been taking a much-needed break together, checking out the high school team to see how they would perform this season.

The following Monday morning after a weekend of mulling over what Nina had shared with me, I enter my tiny office, turn on my computer and quickly read my e-mails. There are no requests for memos or documents from Command Staff, but there is an e-mail from the under-sheriff. He wants to meet with me this afternoon at four o'clock. How strange. What's going on? I rarely interact with him and certainly not in his office on an official appointment. Being way down the chain of command there is no logical reason for us to have such a meeting. When passing in the hallways he has smiled at me and nodded.

Lately however, I became aware that his behavior toward me had changed. He appeared to be frowning as we encountered each other in the hallways. It had all begun right after Nina and I had lunch together. At that time he hadn't even acknowledged us as he usually did. His face had been tense and rigid.

I close out the e-mails. The screen saver comes on. The sounds emanating from the computer are relaxing. Glug, glug, glug. The peaceful sounds of lapping waves flow from the screen. The underwater pictorial is expressing the ocean depths with the shifting of the tides and slow, evocative movement of under-water vegetation. Colorful, tropical creatures are gliding across the ocean floor darting out from behind the bright pieces of seaweed and swirling kelp. I watch transfixed as one tiny pink fish glides swiftly out of the path of a giant aggressive shark. She eludes him, but just barely.

As the day moves on, I write briefs and experience a growing nervousness as the afternoon meeting draws near. I peek in and tell Jim I have a meeting with the under-sheriff at four. He simply nods. Strange, no questions like, "Oh yeah, what about?"

Finally, close to four, I make my way down the hall

through the Records Department.

"Hi Anne, what's up with you today?" queries Gerri, who pulls up most of the telephone transcriptions for our office.

"Well, I'm going to meet with the under-sheriff, Gerri, what do you think of that?'

"Hey, gang," Gerri turns to the Records Staff, "Anne's meeting with the under-sheriff, he's finally talking to the peasants." I join the laughter and continue on thinking, yes, it is unusual for him to speak with a peasant.

The outer office is quiet. Where is Jeanie, the administrative assistant? She is always at her desk. I sit and attempt to calm myself by gazing out the huge plate glass window. The afternoon sun has obliterated all the sparkling slivers of snow. The huge mountains now appear dark and foreboding in their brown barrenness.

The under-sheriff suddenly appears at the door of his office and signals me to enter. The walls are covered with oil paintings of Sioux warriors, perhaps our local Kiowa tribes are too peaceful for him.

His face is inscrutable. Sitting in a wing-backed chair placed directly opposite his desk, I notice he is in his shirt sleeves and apparently delving through a huge pile of paperwork. The door of the office has been closed. We are alone.

I find myself facing another panoramic view of the Rockies immediately behind him. The stark, bright afternoon sun is beginning to edge over the mountains and shines directly into my eyes. I can barely see the under-sheriff, so I shift my position in the chair several times in order to make eye contact.

"Anne, thanks for coming on such short notice. I wanted to inform you we're undergoing budget cuts. I find we're going to have to reevaluate your position."

He looks down at his desk, saying, "You don't seem to have enough responsibilities. We can't keep thinking of more work for you to do. We're running out of ideas. We're going to have to make your position part-time."

I stare at Under-sheriff Hughes in disbelief.

"But sir, we both know I am willing to do more work. I have been churning out more than my share, even performing some of the legal advisor's tasks." I frown realizing he knows this, "If Jim would assign me the work he is supposed to assign me, I would have a time and a half position. The past attorney, Mr. Gaffney, churned out an enormous amount and had a full time paralegal and two interns to boot." I shouldn't have said that. It shows my awareness of a problem they haven't fixed. They still haven't dealt with the issue. Laxity in our office.

The under-sheriff says, "Jim Rice is a very loyal employee."

He stares at me.

I start to fidget.

He repeats, "Jim Rice is extremely loyal and the output of the Legal Advisor's office is another issue, which is not what we're addressing today, Anne." He frowns, "Right now we need to cut back and so your position will be made part-time within two weeks."

My gasp is audible to us both.

"This just isn't fair. What about my benefits?"

"I'm sorry, you'll have to lose your benefits, since you're being switched from full-time to part-time. But that's policy, benefits only go with a full-time position."

"But sir, I need those benefits. I'm a widow. What about my retirement?" I pause. I am close to tears and angry too. "I'm sorry sir, with all due respect, I'm going to have to discuss this with County Human Resources. I need guidance. Half my salary and all my benefits are disappearing with this decision."

He frowns, "I wouldn't advise you to take this matter outside of the office and over to County. County sticks their nose into too much of our business."

He shakes his finger. "Now look, I could terminate your position. You know as well as I do that I'm an 'at-will' employer. You've done a lot of employment law here. You know, I can do whatever I want to do."

Feeling powerless to say anything more, since it would be considered insubordination, I realize I have been silenced. Suddenly I flash back to times in my childhood when my mother ordered me to not "talk back." The disobedient child has been put in her place.

The harsh sun is still shining in my eyes. For a fleeting moment I wonder if the blinds are intentionally open, so I'm made to feel uncomfortable in this setting. I find it difficult to meet the eyes of the under-sheriff. I cannot see. I cannot speak. I begin to notice I am tremoring.

The under-sheriff is staring.

There is a long silence.

"You can go now. You are dismissed."

I rise blindly and edge toward the door.

Making my way back to my office, I seek out Nina, but she's on the phone. I frantically signal her to come see me. She does not look up.

Entering my office I notice the little fish on the computer screen saver is still attempting to flee the huge shark. He snaps at her tiny tail.

Overhearing the loud banging overhead, I realize the deputies upstairs are doing cell checks in the jail. The doors of the cells are clanging away as they swing open and then slam shut. I feel like one of the inmates, powerless, trapped inside of my own personal cell. Suddenly I realize, my cell doors have been very forcefully closed.

Pencil Pushin'

Jebediah Yost's muscles tense under his orange prison jumpsuit as he sits at the sturdy library table. Directly opposite him is wiry Jesse Green. Not a good thing. Jebediah is becoming increasingly irritated as the scratching of Green's pencil on the notebook paper becomes louder and louder. Here we go again, he thinks. Green's playing his usual taunting games.

"Hey dude, your pencil's making too much noise; you're writing too hard on that page, it's bothering me. It's bothering everyone else too."

"So what man, I'm just doing what I'm doing," shoots back Green.

"So quit doing it!"

"Try and stop me," snarls Green.

Jebediah stares him down.

Green glares back at him, but finally shifts his gaze to Jebediah flexing his muscles.

Each week since Jebediah Yost "got shopped" at the Criminal Justice Center, he has been working out on the training equipment. He knows it shows. Not only are the inmates leery of what is happening to him, but he notices even the deputies in Ward 1BA are beginning to glance apprehensively at his burgeoning muscles. The lieutenant has already ordered him a larger jumpsuit.

He has bulked up from 190 to 220 pounds. He is glad. His working out each day and cross-training is keeping him busy and out of trouble with the other inmates. They just sit around at those steel tables in the center of the Mod buzzing like bees amongst themselves, and they sure ain't making no honey. They are up to no good. He has better things to do with his time in here. He is going to become a champion boxer.

Jebediah studies Green. He isn't going to let this low life take him down. He'd keep his cool. He has a future now. Before, when he was selling drugs, that was all there was. He didn't even know what having a future meant. None of the clockers and runners, much less the pipeheads, even thought about a future; all it was about was just moving the product, day in and day out, until you got caught or died. Sure there was a lot of money in it, but you never know when the knockos would come down on you. Those cops had streamlined their procedures. They were out of their cars in an instant doing a shakedown if they smelled trouble. No job security whatsoever. Jebediah had lasted nine months, which was pretty good. He was a careful dude, never wore flashy clothes. He didn't even wear gold chains. No big car. The cops noticed showy things like that. It wasn't smart, drawing attention to yourself with fancy stuff. Besides the money, the only other good thing about the business was the attention you got. When the pipeheads saw you, as you passed by, their eyes lit up. Everybody was glad to see you, man. Even the runners saluted him.

Being a clocker makes you famous. It grows on you. You want more and more attention. And why not?

Pencil Pushin'

Clockers work hard even though it didn't look it. You sit on that park bench, making sure everything works smoothly, timing the arrival and distribution of the drugs. It didn't look much like work, but the whole scenario has to be perfectly tuned. The runners will drive up in their big cars and a stash will be delivered, placed in a littered garbage can. A little kid will pick up the stuff and put it in his lunch box. Then run to an apartment where it is hidden away in a safe place. The old folks really know where to hide the goods, so it can't be found by the cops. Finally it has to be divvied up and distributed to the pipeheads. And it all has to be done before the knockos come. They'd do their shakedowns from four to ten o'clock and then go off to the bars until the end of their shift. Those cops didn't want to be held up by any paperwork past one o'clock in the morning. They wanted to go home.

He remembers the teenage girls sliding up to him, moving in too close, blocking his vision of the runners passing by. They fussed all over him, so he couldn't keep a watch over his business from his park bench. They'd get in his way with their need. He remembers how some of them had been so pretty; now he didn't even want to look at them. It was a damn shame. But even with the pretty ones, in spite of many invitations, Jeb considered clockin' more important than sex.

"Hey, Jeb, how are you doing? Got anything for me?"

"Not yet, wait til' business hours, girl. It's coming."

"We know you'll save some for us. Jebby, you know you got my heart. I'm yours. Got anything extra in the bushes close by?"

"Not now, baby, move on."

Them giving him all that notice made him feel loved for the first time in his life.

But a few weeks ago, Green had ruined all that by turning on him. Not only had that dude, who was now sitting across from him here in the law library, moved in on him and his territory, he had killed his buddy, Collin.

Jebediah seethed as he remembered what the Big Guy, his boss, had said. "You know, Green told me he could move more kilos in your turf than you're moving."

Big Guy had set him up in the trade, taught him everything he knew. He loved Big Guy. What was he about now?

"Sez who?" shot back Jebediah.

"Sez him, Jesse Green," snarled the Big Guy. "You know I'm always wanting to expand the business, Jeb. That's my main game."

"That motherfucker's shooting his mouth off again. I'm moving more kilos than anybody else can. You know that."

"I'm not so sure. I'm going to listen to his plan next time. You know, Jeb, I've got to develop my business. It's called getting the most out of the product. No offense, you're my best clocker, but if Green can do better . . ."

"Big Guy, I am your best clocker and you know it. What you doing here? If you want I'll move five percent more kilos next month and we'll see who's the best."

Big Guy's eyes gleamed.

Because of Green's boasting, Jebediah went looking for him with a baseball bat, but couldn't find him. He found Green's Honda though. He beat the shit out of the car and the sound system. When they heard the sounds of shattered glass, people nearby scattered. They always hid from trouble. For fifteen minutes he concentrated on pummeling the state of the art sound system. At nighttime cruising the streets, Green had played it so loud it disturbed the sleeping little babies. That bastard had no courtesy. Each time he heard the bat hit the metal, Jebediah got madder and madder.

Now, remembering that afternoon, he glares at the little runt across the library table. He sure hates the guy's guts. He decides to ignore his scratchy pencil. He pulls out his sleek, magenta Parker pen and gazes at it fondly. His grandma had given it to him when he got his GED at the Department of Corrections. Well, *she* loves him. She had even made the trip all the way down to Florence. Had come to the graduation ceremony in the big hall. Had his name put on the pen in gold lettering. He twirled the pen now so the gold lettering flashed, but not enough to draw attention to it. He had been very careful about showing it off. If the guards saw it, they'd take it away. The sheriff wanted no potential shanks in the jail.

Jesse is glaring at him. Good! "Hey, that flashing getting in my eyes, it's bothering me," complains Green.

"So what! You're bothering me," says Jebediah.

"I got to get this pleading done, man."

"So do I, man."

"You should be more considerate. I'm going to report you have that pen to one of the deps."

Jebediah laughs, "You report me, just try it. He shook his pen at Green. "Look dude, you and me got a lot of issues here. We got to work them out."

"Issues, what's this issue shit? What you talking bout?" asked Green.

"I'm talking bout getting along and talking about our issues."

"Who you been talking to, that psycho therpist? He's all into fooling with your head."

"He's helping me to think better, make better decisions," shoots back Jebediah.

Jesse laughs, "Oh man, you've been had, if you believe that stuff."

"Knock it off, you dudes," roars old grizzly Ray Jones from the adjacent table. "You guys don't start nothing in here, you hear? Miz LePon will report all of us. We'll lose our library privileges." He shakes his finger at them. "You know how hard it is to get time in here. What are you both thinking? My court date's next week. I've got to finish this for the judge, so shut your fucking mouths."

"Whoa, you telling me to shut my fucking mouth?" snarls Green.

"Yeah! What's it to you? Listen, I want to get out of here. I don't know about you, Green. You're just wanting to make trouble. Shut the fuck up. Shut your mouth."

"Scuse me, say what?"

Jones bends over his work muttering, "Motherfucker."

Silence ensues. They all seem grateful for that. The room is small enough as it is and they are packed in too close. There are five of them squeezed in here; the motherfucker Green, old mangy Jones, him, and two new inmates who are learning the legal ropes. They all turn back to concentrating on their legal pleadings.

Jebediah takes pride in how well he can research cases. He spends half his time in here, begging God each time to help him find a way to get the judges to release him. It gives him a sense of control just like the working out does.

Miz LePon, the paralegal, told him that years ago judges had mandated a section of each criminal justice center be set aside for inmates to work on their cases. At that time the sheriff had grudgingly consented to set up this tiny room off the laundry room as a law library. And later on he had added amenities such as a copier. They were even being trained on computers. They could be heard guiding each other in the Mod during meals as to what legal citations to use.

Some of them, like the old timer, Jones, were really good at it. He had lots of practice. He could find the correct cites of cases in just a few minutes while it took the new inmates hours. Three walls of the law library were lined from top to bottom with legal books. Any attorney in private practice would be proud to have those books in his law office. The fourth wall contained a large picture window. Miz LePon, the law librarian, not only assisted them with research, she also could keep an eye on them through the window and if there was any trouble, she could call a deputy.

Jebediah glances about. The two new inmates are squished in at the other table; Larry Bean and Joe Beach have heaps of books all over it. They hadn't narrowed their citations down yet. Funny, even though they are both in for burglary, here in this room they appear scholarly as they shuffle through the *Pacific Reporters*.

Because his attention is being drawn to the scratchy

pen, he is getting madder and madder. Jebediah uses the therpist's suggestion and decides to think of a nice time in the past. He isn't going to pay no attention to this scum bag. He is going to do his work. He has a goal. Old Jones is right, he thinks, Green is nothing but a troublemaker. He focuses his thoughts on his grandma. She is so proud of him. She says no one in the family has graduated from high school before. Well, it wasn't a real graduation from high school, but just the same, she thought it was. His momma didn't care. She had thrown him out of her place months ago in a show down about his drug dealing. She wanted nothing to do with him. His grandma had visited him every week since he had been here. She had driven over after the Baptist church services every Sunday. Boy, did she look like something else when she appeared. Last Sunday she was in a yellow daffodil dress with a hat that matched. It was so big, she couldn't get through the scanner at the entrance. The Deps got her all flustered up by making her take off the wide rimmed hat. She was mad as hell.

"What those guys making trouble for a grandma in her Sunday best for?"

"Now Grandma, they got rules here."

"Well, I don't think they show no respect. It's Sunday. You'd think they'd be more respectful on Sunday."

"Pay no mind to them, Grandma." He changes the subject, "You still got my cash safe and sound?"

"I keep it all in the oven."

"What the hell, Grandma? What if someone turns on the oven? How much you got in there?"

It's all there, one hundred thousand, I count the bundles every night. Well, except the five hundred you told me to take out each month for me, Sugar. It's safe, who would think to look in an oven for money? You know, you're not the only smart one in the family."

"Find another spot. Someone's going to light that oven some day and then where will we be?"

"No one else uses that oven, and you know I don't cook."

"Tell you what, Grandma, you help yourself to three thousand more of that money and promise me you'll find another place for the rest, okay?"

Hearing the "three thousand" mentioned, she glowingly nods.

"What about using a safety deposit box?"

"I don't trust no bank teller. They might take the money and lock me in the vault."

"Well, buy a safe at Sears then, and put it in the cellar."

* * * * *

As he sits at the library table, he stares down at her gift. Sure is a lucky pen. It had helped him. That night after Collin died, he wrote with it in his journal. He had learned to journal keep from the psycho therpist. It eases his mind. He has had to write in it often since Collin passed on. He couldn't get his mind off it.

He and Collin went back a long way. The psycho therpist said he and Collin had bonded over the years. They were like brothers. They went way back to Vietnam. He couldn't forget the Battle of Hue. It still kept botherin.' Every night he could hear Collin calling and calling for him. That night on the fifteenth day of the Tet offensive, the Cong were hitting them with every piece of artillery they had. They had been ordered to pull back.

"Hey, Jeb, when you coming man? I'm hit Jeb, bleeding bad. Can't move my leg to get up. Come on out here. Where are you dude?" It went on for hours and hours, the whimpering; Jeb was beside himself.

For some reason as crazy as it was, Collin had stood up to take a leak and got his leg shot out from under him. Jeb heard the lieutenant order them to retreat and pleaded with him for permission to help Collin, but the lieutenant said follow orders, the medics would get Collin. And they finally did, but at that time Jebediah felt he had let Collin down.

* * * * *

And now it was even worse because he had let him down again. Big Guy had talked Jebediah into working with Jesse Green as a team. Big Guy said maybe teaming up would bring in more money. So one night in Jebediah's Grandma's apartment, the three of them, Green, Collin and him were mixing and measuring the stuff. It was after the knockos' hours around one o'clock in the morning, so they felt safe. They knew the cops were probably down at Duffy's drinking before they went home.

But the three heard the hoot, hoot, hoot of an owl through the kitchen window. That was the signal someone was in the neighborhood who shouldn't be. There sure weren't no owls in the projects. They stared at each other and listened harder. They heard the front door shut softly and then a rustling at the back of the building. Was that the sound of a footstep on the stairs?

Pencil Pushin'

"Man, oh man, they're coming," hissed Collin.

"How'd they know we were here?" asked Green. Jebediah eyed him suspiciously and thought, yeah, how'd they know?

"Who cares," he said. "Get this fucking stuff out of here."

Green frantically poured the stash into Jebediah's grandma's washing machine and turned it on. Their eyes bulged as they watched the coke swish around in the water.

Collin was chopping up hose with a kitchen knife and putting the rest of the paraphernalia behind the garbage can under the sink.

Jebediah rushed out to the back pantry placing the now empty Coke bottles, used for storing the stuff, in the bottle rack.

"They're going to find it. They're going to find it!"

"Shut up Collin, don't be stupid," whispered Jebediah.

Green got out cigars and the cards and started dealing as fast as he could. On the kitchen counter, Jebediah spotted five extra condoms filled with cocaine, which Green had set aside for a special customer.

"And what about these?" he asked Green.

"I don't know, brother." He tossed them at Collin in desperation.

"Do what you've got to do, Collin," hissed Green.

There was a knock.

Collin stood there, thought for a moment, and then gulped down all five condoms.

Jebediah tried to stop him. "Buddy don't do that, it ain't worth it."

"Sometimes it works," said Collin.

"Well, well, you boys playing cards and doing Grandma's laundry? How nice," said the head knocko as he slammed through the door. Four more knockos rushed in and started the search.

Now thinking back, Jebediah kept remembering how bad it was. He hadn't slept much since just thinking on it. They had been strip searched, photographed, fingerprinted and led to their cells. Jebediah had been placed directly across the Mod from Collin. Collin hadn't passed the cocaine filled condoms. He could hear him on the can trying to pass it all. Toward morning Jebediah heard him whimpering and saw him hunched over.

"Jebediah, help me," cried Collin across the Mod.

"I'm getting you some help, hang on, brother."

He waited fifteen minutes until the deputy passed by him making the rounds of cell checks. "Dep, something's wrong with my friend over there. He's all bent over."

Sgt. Rafferty went over, opened up the cell and called over to the desk deputy, "Call medical right away. This doesn't look right."

A minute later the door to the Mod slammed and a nurse appeared. The sergeant showed her into the cell. Jedediah saw her taking Collin's blood pressure. Taking the blood pressure? Must not be good. Had the cocaine gotten into Collin's blood stream?

The nurse rose and ordered, "Call the hospital. Get him down to the Sally Port as quickly as possible. Code Blue, Blue!"

Bells rang. Deputies rushed in. The heartbeat was

checked. It was weak. Pulse weak. An IV was put in.

The nurse saw Jebediah watching. She approached his cell.

"You know what might be wrong with him?"

"I think he ate something didn't agree with him."

"Oh yeah, what was it?"

"Cocaine."

"Jesus, it's probably gotten into his bloodstream, his blood pressure is really low. I think it's too late. Why didn't you tell someone?"

"He made me promise not to."

Jebediah watched as they wheeled Collin away on a gurney.

* * * * *

Now, in the law library, Jebediah put his grandma's pen to paper. Shiny pen, help me write the words to get me out of this fucking place. *United States v. Jeffers 342 US 48.* He is using that citation to support his own case. He is up for possession of cocaine. The cops had searched his grandma's place for the coke and hadn't had a warrant. This case is almost like what happened to him. Another dude, a clocker, had stored his stash with his aunts in a hotel. The house detective had been told there was some stuff in the hotel room and had reported it to the police. The police entered the hotel room without a warrant, searched it and seized the narcotics. It was determined in the original court case that the narcs could use the evidence in court. But on appeal the good old judge reversed it, saying with no warrant it violated the defendant's constitutional rights and they couldn't use it. The clocker got off. Maybe he'd get lucky and have the same judge hearing his case if it went up for appeal.

He can see Miz LePon through the big window. She seems real busy today. She usually kept a careful watch on them. Right now it looks like she had stepped out of her office, probably to go down to the Sally Port to accept a delivery of legal books. She has been real nice, getting this cite for him. The sheriff's paralegal is older, grandmotherly. She is teaching them how to research their cases in the computer. They use Lexis, for their research, just like big time lawyers. Those legal computer programs could pull up a lot of cases and print them out. In the past, the paralegal wrote him notes on his requests telling him which cases were reliable and which were not. It was nice of her to do that. Why are old people so nice? His grandma and the paralegal?

Jebediah looks up and sees old mangy Jones hunched over his work. He is a pro at legal work. He had been in and out of this place so often he knew all the legalese. He is ready to go to court next week and his papers are carefully placed in a small binder ready to send over to the judge. He has a large sheath of folders he has spent weeks on. He looks up and grins at Jebediah as he pats his folder with satisfaction. He gets up and takes his brief into Miz. LePon's sound-proof booth. She is looking it over very carefully and checking the cites in the computer in the rear of her office.

Jebediah stares at Green. He notices the sound of Green's pencil getting louder and louder. Is he trying to start something again? Everybody else has stopped writing. They are looking at him and Green. They are watch-

Pencil Pushin'

ing the pencil moving across the page. It is quiet. Jebediah senses all eyes latched on him. Watching. Waiting. Green keeps pushing that pencil. They all seem fascinated by the movement of his hand. Green begins to move his eraser at the end of the pencil back and forth, back and forth across the page. Soon there is a large clump of erasure right across from Jebediah.

Jebediah is trying to get control of his festering feelings. He thinks, I'd better calm myself or I'll lose it. He focuses on the pen. Tries to concentrate on his Grandma's pride in him. He thinks about Collin dying in here for nothing. He wants to do good for them both. Suddenly, with one wide sweep of the arm, Green brushes the bits of erasure across his page on to Jebdiah's papers.

Jebediah stands up shrieking in rage. It is too much.

"What the fuck did you do that for? You're pushing me as far as you're ever going to push me."

With that he heaves up the edge of the table and slams it against Green pinning him against the book case on the far wall. Pen, pencils, papers and books go flying. Scrawny Larry Bean ducks out of range down behind the copier over in the far corner.

Green, whose eyes fill with fear says, "I didn't mean it. I didn't mean it."

"Like hell you didn't."

And with the flat of his hand he starts to smack Green's face again and again as he wedges him against the wall behind the table.

"Do you think I'm dumb or something? Why the hell you do that crazy thing?"

His thick, broad hand goes smack, smack, smack.

"It's pay back time for all you done to me and Collin. You killed him. And you tried to weasel in on my territory."

"So what? You weren't selling that much anyway."

Enraged by this, Jebediah switches to fists. Blood is beginning to spatter in every direction. Green's head swings back and forth.

Joe Beach is bobbing around in back of the other table yelling, "Give it to him good, Jebbie, give it to him good."

Splat, splat.

"You killed Collin, you killed Collin," he chants in time to the beat of his fists.

Jebediah sees blood all over his hands. Messy. He wipes them on his jumpsuit and starts in again. Green's face is pulp.

Out of the corner of his eye, Jeb sees old Jones rush in to clutch the rest of his legal briefs protectively to his chest. Blood is splattering all over.

Jones is shaking his head back and forth in disgust muttering. "This is no good, this is no good." He inches over to the thick window, pounding loudly, "Miz LePon, Miz LePon, Code Red, Code Red." he screams at her.

She looks up from her legal book, pales, and reaches frantically for the jail alarm button, shouting into the intercom, "Code Red! Code Red!"

Jebediah is thinking of Collin as he keeps beating up on Green. This is the way I can get even for Collin, and make the world right. As the sounds of a fist hitting cheek bones grows with more rapidity, outside the room he can hear the sounds of the thick double doors slamming and bells going off. The thumping of boots resounds down the hallway. The walls of the building shake as the thumping draws nearer. He hears the lieutenant shouting orders.

There is a pause.

Absolute silence.

Jebediah releases his grip on Green and lets him slide to the floor. Best I make myself into a lump. *It's best to be a lump now.*

He looks down at Green covered with blood. Green's moaning is weaker and weaker. Good, he hopes he'd killed the motherfucker. The door bursts open suddenly. The black garbed Special Operations Removal Team enters quickly. A closely packed wedge of black uniformed humanity moves across the room in tight formation.

"Yost, you're not going to give us any trouble are you? Let's make this easy."

"No sir, I'm making it easy. Never caused any trouble before have I?"

"No you haven't," responds the lieutenant. "Team advance."

The team comes at him full force. He does not resist. They place him on the cement floor. Each take a position surrounding him. They quickly remove his prison jumpsuit. Jebediah lays nude, face up, watching them apprehensively. They cuff his hands behind his back and place the leg shackles on. He can't move. He is helpless. Lying there naked. He looks up at the hidden faces behind the black shields attached to the helmets. What will they do next? The team rises and stands back.

Jebediah can hear Jones screaming at him, "My brief is covered with blood. You ruined my brief, you motherfucker. You ruined everything for all of us. Why'd you do it?"

The lieutenant orders, "Jones, quit your yammering. I'm ordering you to go over to the desk sergeant's station and give him your say-so about what happened here. Your brief will be okay."

"No it won't, Lieutenant, the work of a legal intellectual is destroyed, covered with Green's blood. I'm going to sue the jail. You're supposed to keep this place safe. It's just like being out on the streets in here," Jones shakes his head ruefully.

The lieutenant looks at him in disgust. "Okay, all the rest of you, the party's over. Go to your cells for lockdown. Rafferty, escort them to their respective cells."

He motions to another member of the special removal team. "Call Medical and get them down here. There's probably not much they can do for this face. Team, take places."

The four remaining members of Special Operations Team take their places surrounding Jebediah. There is a sudden glinty flash emanating from his hand.

"Hold it one minute, what have we here? A pen! Let me have that, Yost."

Jebediah, hesitates, then offers up the pen. What will he do without his grandma's pen?

"Team, commence," orders the lieutenant.

The four remaining members of SORT pick up the naked Jebediah like a side of beef. Each is assigned an extremity, one for each leg and one for each arm. They edge towards the door.

"Place him in Isolation."

When they pass the paralegal's window, Jeb's eyes lock on Miz LePon's. She is wringing her hands and shaking her head.

As Jebediah is carried down the long hall toward Isolation, all he can think is how much he wants his Grandma's pen.

El Paso County, Colorado

Mixed Signals

As Lucy eases herself down on to the soft cushions on the sturdy wooden pew, she notices the ache in her back again. It's not going away. It's been there for forty years, an early auto accident; her expectations of it getting better are wildly off base. Oh well, she thinks, so much for the premise of the golden years. But church is a source of comfort in dealing with the ensuing twilight. Approaching the winter season of life comes the loss of one's physical abilities: a faltering step, a squinting of the eyes when encountering the printed word, a loss of experiencing the zestiness of food, a slowness in rising, a leaning forward to better hear. The diminishing of all of these physical attributes is disconcerting, but the necessary compromises on one's part have to be made.

Since Lucy hasn't attended church lately, she studies the new renovations. The changes reflect the taste of those who have sought to evoke a subtle, devotional, atmosphere. The use of a rather soft bisque for the interior walls with an edging of maroon to offset the architectural feature of faux arches offers a sense of peace. Certainly nothing too startling or too blatant. The huge sanctuary still retains a majestic presence with its vast, high ceilings. It is one of the major churches in Colorado Springs, which some consider to be the church capital of the world. Behind the altar, the color selection of soft muted green evokes a sense of serenity.

She gazes over the congregation, most of them gray hairs like herself. The women dressed in soft pastels or flowery prints. None too bright or showy. The men in bright, colorful blazers with comfortable linen slacks. She knows many of them, their smiles, reassurances and interests. All reliable and predictable, just like the service every Sunday. She has attended the Methodist Church since she was a little girl and the ritual, hymns and sermons were always similar, never changing. The sameness is somewhat reassuring.

As Lucy looks about, her attention is suddenly drawn to a nice looking gentlemen striding up the church aisle. He appears to be smiling directly at her. She turns to look at the folks in the pew behind her to see if his gaze is directed at them. It's just Amy Hitchcock. Was the smile directed at her? Looking down for a moment, she glances up again to check him out. He appears to want to catch her eye. He is short in stature, rather dapper, wearing a gray pin stripe suit and rep tie. His well-shod feet are encased in shoes so polished, they gleam. She later learns he was an aircraft carrier fighter pilot in World War II; the spit and polish is probably due to military discipline. She doesn't know what to make of this unexplained attention toward her, but she smiles shyly in return. He circles around the rear of the church and comes back down the center aisle sitting at the opposite end of her pew. No one sits between them. As the prelude begins, she glances in his direction to study him more carefully. He is tan, wears glasses and reminds her of the impish diminutive Winston Churchill. The congregation rises for the opening anthem; he looks up from his hymnal and glances over at her with a slight grin. She again returns the smile, but quickly looks down.

At the end of service, he moves across the pew toward her, "Oh, my dear lady, I am so happy to see you in church. You're finally here," he exclaims.

She hesitates a moment, uncertain of what he means. Has she met him? Is her hearing loss betraying her again? Is she misunderstanding? But he seems to know her or is at least is giving the impression he knows about her.

She pauses and after a moment, catching on to what might actually be occurring she responds, "Well, thank you, it's good to be here, I haven't attended services lately. I enjoyed the sermon. Did you?'

"Oh, yes, I always profit from Phillip's sermons."

Feeling rather awkward with not knowing what to say next, she turns in slight desperation to draw Amy Hitchcock into the conversation. Amy has sat in the pew behind her for ten years. Grinning, Amy jumps right in. She apparently knows him and greets him by name. As the three engage in polite chitchat, Lucy makes every effort to be as pleasing as possible. She hasn't caught on to his name, but refers to him, when directing her conversation to both of them as "This nice gentlemen," smiling as appealingly as she can, hoping she's not spreading herself too thick.

When he leaves, Amy reaches over and takes Lucy's arm. She whispers, "Tom is perfectly charming isn't he?"

Lucy nods in agreement.

Amy continues, "And such a good church person. We

don't have enough good church folks like Tom. He's in charge of administering the church's budget, you know. He gathers in the financial sheaves, so to speak." She looks at Lucy intently and adds an aside, "He's been a widower for ten years, we wonder about that," raising her eyebrows

Lucy backs away and gives Amy a slight wave goodbye. What was that last comment about? Was it meant to be a warning?

The following Sunday, anticipating she might see him again, Lucy dresses for church with great care, even putting on eyeliner, which is a feat for her, since she can't see well enough without her glasses to do an adequate job. For accessories she sets aside her grandmother's rope pearls and the scarab bracelet her late husband gave her when they were courting back in the fifties. She wears her loose fitting navy suit with navy purse and shoes to match. In retrospect, a few months later, she realizes she chose the dress for success look she had been so accustomed to, rather than a feminine outfit. Lucy was sure Tom was old school as far as women were concerned.

Arriving very early for church services, she chooses to sit in her usual place. Will he show? While anxiously waiting for whatever might happen, she listens to the prelude. Bach. Thank goodness. At the Presbyterian Church a few blocks down, they feature Pop music. Poor misguided souls.

She becomes distracted. Her attention is drawn to the conversation of two ladies sitting in front of her. Babble, babble, babble. She senses they are probably close friends and have seen each other only yesterday, so what do they have to talk about? It never ceases to amaze her how many people use this time for personal conversation rather than saying their prayers and directing their thoughts to the Heavenly Father. She's talked to the senior pastor about it, but he counseled her about times changing and the need for the church to adapt to new ways. She left her minister with a dry comment of, "Oh pastor, my, oh my, what a serious mistake."

Here comes Tom. It's happening again. Could he really be interested in her? It's been so many years since she's received male attention, at least that she's been aware of. She's developed a habit of filtering it out.

He strides up the aisle giving her a broad smile and circles around the back. She returns his smile. Tom's repeating last Sunday's performance. There has to be intent here. Today he is wearing a navy pin-striped suit with a rep tie and blue oxford cloth shirt. With satisfaction, she notices his appearance again denoting a businesslike sensibility. It is comforting. Rather than appearing overly friendly, she prohibits herself from gazing in his direction too often and studies the altar decorations for this Sunday's service. Two large celadon vases of white spider chrysanthemums form a pyramid with spiky tendrils reaching up toward the stark gold cross. The tendrils seem to be reaching upward toward the heavens, stretching for something inexplicably elusive. The cross is typical of Protestant crosses. There is the absence of the figure of Christ hanging upon it and certainly no indication of the broken, suffering Savior.

The opening hymn begins, "Be still my soul, the Lord is on your side." How prophetic. She certainly has a need to sing this particular song, since her nerves are so on edge as she attempts to anticipate what might happen next. But much to her disappointment, nothing does. There is no conversation after services. No connection. His attention seems to be focused upon others. He must be attending to church business. As she drives home, down the wide familiar tree-lined streets of the Old North End, she feels dispirited. Has she misinterpreted the signals? She pushes the button on the DVD player, Kiri Te Kanawa singing *Tosca*. As Lucy listens to what she considers the most beautiful operatic female aria, she thinks, yes, I feel just like Tosca, I attend church regularly and pray regularly, but where are the rewards?

The following weeks roll by and the Sunday pattern persists; the grin, the smiles, as Tom makes his way up the aisle, but again no conversation. At one service a tiny elderly woman sits between them, hampering any smiles or glances. And then unfortunately the next Sunday, Sally Brinkley, a friend of hers, places herself between them, saying she would enjoy having Lucy's company during the service. Thus, there is no opportunity for any interaction between Lucy and Tom. She could strangle Sally.

Six Sundays after their initial encounter with the glad smile, the winks, but no direct connection, Lucy becomes increasingly frustrated. Shouldn't we be drawing closer, she wonders. He smiles at her so warmly, doesn't that signal his interest? Deciding to take matters into her own hands, arriving home after services, she summons the courage to look up his phone number in the church directory and galvanizing her courage, she dials.

"Hello, Tom, Mr. Wentworth, this is Lucy Selby calling. I sit in church in the same pew as you."

"Oh hello, Lucy, yes, of course, I enjoyed conversing with you a while ago."

"Well, I'm sort of in a pickle, I seem to have lost my glasses and am retracing my steps in order to find them. Did you happen to notice a pair of glasses left in the pew yesterday?"

"No, I don't believe I did, but I wasn't looking, really."

"Oh dear, yes, I guess I'll have to replace them, they are prescription glasses and a bit expensive."

"I might suggest you see the church receptionist at the front desk before you do take that step, your glasses might have been turned in there."

"Oh, thank you for your advice, I'll do just that. Well, I won't trouble you any further, thanks again. Tallyho."

She hangs up, "Tallyho. Where had she gotten that ridiculous phrase, "Tallyho." She has never used that expression in her life. But at least, she has broken the ice. The festering feelings of waiting it out have dissipated.

The next Sunday, she sees him before services in the hallway and as he passes, says, "Oh, Tom Wentworth, good morning. Guess what? I found my glasses in my two year old grandson's toy box."

He shakes his head. "I doubt that," and moves on.

"Oh," she flounders, and then immediately speeds off. Has she heard him correctly? What a cutting remark. Stinging from that unexpected response, she huddles in the pew and ponders his abrupt rejoinder. Is it her hearing again, did she misinterpret? Was his remark really that cutting? Should she take it as a signal to buzz off?

Suddenly, just a few moments later, there he is, striding up the aisle and again giving her that warm welcoming look. As if nothing had happened. So we're back to square one. I don't understand what's going on here. These waters are truly murky. I'll have to wait for more signals. Damnation, why do I have to wait? He's not playing by the rules. Does Tom know the rules? But then again, she isn't familiar with the rules either. It's been so long.

After services she eases across the pew toward him. The look of a trapped animal flashes across his face. She ignores it, and sits down next to him and says, "Tom, I understand, you're a poet."

"Yes, I am. In fact, I have written a book of poetry."

"Really, that's wonderful! Well I don't know if you are aware, but our Sunday School class, Kerygma, has a writing group, would you be interested in joining it? We have some members writing memoirs, another is writing a young adult book, I write short stories. You would offer our group another dimension, I mean, to have a poet on board. Would you like to join us?

"Well, that might be rather nice. Who is in it? When do you meet?"

While filling him in on the details, she displays her baby blues to advantage, as she pauses and looks up at him.

He moves closer, "Yes, I think I would like to come."

"I'm thrilled you'd like to join us. We meet at Montague's, the tea house on Tejon, every Saturday morning at nine. We'll see you next week then."

The following Saturday as she enters Montague's, he

glows at her. He seems to be happy in the group. She discovers his poetry is really quite good. But she learns something else.

"I never revise a poem," he announces to the other writers.

"You don't?"

"No, once it's written, that's it. It's perfect as it is."

There are questioning looks. Those who systematically struggle with multiple revisions appear to be inwardly festering.

"Wow, I understand Donald Hall, the poet laureate, had revised one of his eight line poems 498 times," Sam Howe says as he shakes his bald head. "And you don't have to revise? That's incredible!"

"I simply jot mine down and they're done. I like them just as they are."

He is so sure of himself. She hides her true thoughts, by responding, "How fortunate for you." A few who have gotten her veiled comeuppance smile at her secretly.

The espresso machine goes off right at this point and since some of them have hearing problems, the conversation ceases for a moment.

As they leave and they always manage to leave together after each session, she asks him how long it has been since his wife passed on.

"Ten years ago. She was French, you know."

No, she didn't know.

"Ten years, that seems like quite a while."

He shakes his head, "No I don't think so, it seems just like yesterday. It was a roller coaster of a marriage, though, lots of passion."

She laughs, "How metaphorical, to describe a marriage as a roller coaster with its ups and downs."

Tom smiles.

"Mine was too. A real roller coaster of a ride," she laments.

He smiles and leans closer and looks at her directly. "I'm going to take a trip to Paris and then down the Loire on a barge this summer. It might be difficult, bringing back all those memories of Ellen, but I feel a need to reconnect with her, we're drawing apart."

Lucy hearing this looks at Tom uncertainly.

He says reassuringly, "I have a habit of talking to her all the time, but she seems to be disappearing on me. I'll be gone the entire month of June. Then, I'll be back to start out afresh." He looks at Lucy intently.

She simply nods, not knowing how to respond. All of a sudden she wants to grab him and shake him. This means she'll have to wait another month. Lordy, such fierceness. What's come over her?

As she edges her car out of the parking lot, she wonders, ten years! Ten years and he hasn't gotten over it? Is it possible to mourn for ten years?

Through May, the pattern of their pas de deux continues with the striding up the aisle, the flashing smiles, but now at the end of services, there is only polite chit-chat. Finally the last Sunday in May, he eases over and sits down on the plush pew cushion next to her. This is a first, she thinks. A change. He has only once moved towards her side of the pew. Was this it? An invitation to go out for coffee? A bit of lunch? A drink at the Broadmoor?

He looks quite serious as he leans towards her, "As I told you, I'll be gone the next month. I'm off to France, I'll be back in July."

She nods mutely. She'll be darned if she's going to wish him well.

Surprisingly, the month passes quickly. The six grandchildren are over often to swim in the pool. She and her daughter laugh uproariously at their pranks. She takes pride in their glowing, healthy bodies glistening in the sunshine. The sounds of "Marco, Polo, . . . Marco Polo," reach into the kitchen as she prepares their egg salad sandwiches.

July at last. She dresses with great care. She eases into her soft powder blue three piece crepe suit. She has lost ten pounds. The summer sun has lightened her hair to a soft shade of blonde. She feels she's at her best.

Upon entering the sanctuary, she sees him sitting in his usual seat. It's a change in the pattern. He is not striding up the aisle with a warm smile. She slowly walks down and eases into her side of the pew looking in his direction. Tom does not glance her way. No smile, no wink, no gesture. He appears to be reading his Bible.

As the organist begins the prelude, she attempts to concentrate on the music. The congregation rises to sing the anthem. Tom casts no smile in her direction at the beginning of the hymn. Sitting there pondering, she wonders, what's happening? Is this it? All the attention and encounters are for naught? Perhaps he's waiting until after services to speak with her. She finds it difficult to concentrate upon the universal theme of the sermon, "Do unto others as you would have them do unto you." The closing anthem is sung. Benediction is said. She looks over in Tom's direction. He is gone. Disappeared. She sits down in the pew to catch her breath. The church begins to empty out. She hears the muffled sounds of the remaining voices in the foyer. She huddles there alone, sinking lower into the soft cushions. Hearing footsteps, she expectantly turns. It is just the ushers cleaning up the pews. She begins to shiver. She draws her crepe suit jacket closer about her, but the chill persists. She notices the ache in her back from prolonged sitting has returned. Funny, she hasn't been aware of it in the past few months. She sighs. She slowly rises and makes her way up the church aisle. As she walks out into the gray overcast day, the mood of her despair matches the dreary, colorless sky. It is over, she thinks, and it hadn't even begun.

Good Church People

"Who are these people?" Hazel demands in her churlish voice. "How did they get into our Shakespeare Group? I don't recognize their e-mail names. Do they go to our church? Are they good church people?"

As Lucy shifts the phone receiver to her good ear, she thinks they could be "good church people" if you, Hazel, and a few others would make them feel welcome. But, as usual, when she listens to Hazel, Lucy begins to fold right away. Hazel's persistent droning on and on wears people down. Lucy is quite sure no amount of discussion is going to change Hazel's reasoning. Hazel has been program chairman of the Sunday school group for many years and has managed to offend many with her bullheadedness. Lucy can just picture her on the other end of the line with her beady black eyes flashing and her bright scarlet lips clenched. She is probably shaking her metallic, helmet-like tresses with vivid animation. Although Lucy doubts it's possible for Hazel's tresses to move at all, since the gold and silver tint seems to be lacquered on like shellac.

Lucy wishes she could respond, "Hazel, these folks are some of the best intellectuals in Colorado Springs. Why, Professor Thomas, who taught Shakespeare at Colorado College for twenty years and is a world renowned scholar, is the most patient, kind, and gentle. person in the world. Who could be more Christian?"

Instead, Lucy chooses to do as she has in the past in regard to conversations with Hazel, she gives up too readily. So much for Lucy's investment of one thousand dollars worth of classes in assertions skills. She thinks back to stock phrases such as "I'm uncomfortable with what you're saying" and the ultimate, "I just don't agree with you." None of these assertive phrases would have worked with Hazel.

"What would you suggest I do, Hazel? These folks are now very much a part of our Shakespeare Sunday school group and are invaluable in sharing their knowledge with us. They are loved and respected. I'm not going to ask them to leave the group, that would hurt them and considering their expertise, it would be insulting."

Hazel bears down, saying, "Lucy, we just can't have these non-members be a part of a Sunday school group. It can't be done. You'll have to think of some other solution."

"Like what? What would you suggest, Hazel?" Lucy suddenly realizes here is where she is making a big mistake, opening it up to Hazel.

"Leave."

"Leave? Have the entire group leave the Sunday School? Don't you think that's a little harsh?" Feeling utterly deflated at Hazel's demands, Lucy sinks down on her chintz-flowered bedspread. All her stamina has been sucked out of her. She is getting too old for these power plays. She studies her reflection in the gold, gilt-edged mirror across the room. Gracious, her blonde wavy hair is in disarray. She evidently has been nervously fiddling with it as she has been speaking with Hazel. She looks as if she's been in a wind tunnel.

Hazel's voice shoots up a decibel, "Well, we have to abide by the rules, you know. They are not members and actually, Lucy," she pauses, "I never really understood the connection between Shakespeare and religion."

"Listen, Hazel, Shakespeare used numerous references to the Bible in his plays. Look at *King Lear;* there are at least thirteen references to Biblical passages.

"Well, there is just so much violence in them."

"As you and I both well know, Hazel, there's more violence in the Bible, than in Shakespeare's plays. The good book is filled with violent aggressive characters. Look at God; in the Old Testament, he used violence whenever he was unhappy with what was going on in the world." She shifts the receiver getting a second wind, "And besides think of the great moral lessons Shakespeare teaches. Look at the *Merchant of Venice* with its 'quality of mercy' soliloquy."

"Well, I don't want to diddle around about the Bible and Shakespeare anymore. We have rules. The group will just have to leave. That's it."

As Hazel prattles on, Lucy tunes her out. Her attention is drawn to the action in the birdfeeder just outside her bedroom window. A huge black crow is nudging the bright little yellow gold finches off the thistle-filled feeder with his large sharp beak. He persistently pushes and pushes at them. Lucy wants to go and bang on the window to scare him off, but she's hooked to the phone with that droning voice at the end of the line. Her attention returns to the conversation, if you can call it a conversation, it's so one-sided. What to do, what to do. She ponders?

Finally, and she has no idea where her gumption comes from, she draws herself up off the bed, squares her shoulders and responds, "You know, Hazel, now that I given it some more thought as I've listened to you, your solution is rather appropriate." She continues in her most forceful voice, "If these genuine, highly respected people, who share their knowledge and fellowship with us are not going to be made to feel welcome in the Shakespeare group, then for me to argue with you is a moot point. Why would I insist upon having them remain, when they are going to be made uncomfortable in our 'Christian' setting? Actually it's an oxymoron."

"What do you mean? What does moot point and oxymoron mean?"

"Hazel, look those words up in the dictionary."

"I don't have time. Explain it to me. You're the wordy person," Hazel demands.

"Sorry Hazel, I've got to run. I have to phone the members of the Shakespeare group and explain what has happened. This isn't going to be well received by some. And I shall make certain they are made aware this is your decision, not mine. In the meantime, I would suggest you, yourself look up the word 'oxymoron' and while you're at it look up the word 'Christian.' It might do you some good."

As Lucy not too gently puts down the receiver, she hears Hazel's unrelenting voice continuing. She smiles as she looks in her gold-framed mirror on the far bedroom wall and thinks, you outfoxed her, you smart old lady. That will show her. But she hadn't outfoxed Hazel, and now she was faced with having to make some very hurtful phone calls.

Isabelle Weir

Isabelle Weir is not a study in motion. Early in the morning she is often found propped up in bed knitting or watching the morning news. She rises at five-thirty. Can't help herself. For most of her life she has had to be out early to earn her daily bread. On Sunday mornings she might bury herself in the local paper for an hour, which is a feat, since the local newspaper, *The Gazette's* news coverage is the size of a pin.

After breakfast she ventures out on to her townhouse patio in a brightly colored Muumuu and yellow Crocs to tend her plants and check out the neighbors. As she turns on the garden hose full force, the pungent scent from the needles of the surrounding Austrian pines greets her. What a way to start the day. She checks for her friends, the furry squirrels, in order not to douse them. They are always present since she feeds them prodigious amounts of peanuts. This causes great consternation among the nearby neighbors, who find the profusion of squirrels less than amusing. This morning, she shoos them away and commences to overwater everything: her sun-shy impatiens, sturdy begonias, lightly scented lavender, soft-leafed foxglove, and double-blossomed petunias. With the exception of the lavender, all the blossoms are white. Whenever a full moon appears, she sits on her patio in the evenings, sips a glass of white wine and gazes upon the lustrous white blossoms, illuminated by spheres of the lunar soft, white light.

Going about her morning tasks, she not only causes an inclination for all the flora she has doused to drown, but this daily ritual also results in the neighbors gritting their teeth as she runs up the communal water bill. She doesn't care, in fact she enjoys driving the neighbors crazy, especially those directly across the way. Between them, there now exists a three year running feud, which came about after they began to lay down bricks extending their patio, encroaching upon all the neighbors in the area. Isabelle immediately reported this breach to the association board. It was her civic duty. Talk about territorial hubris! She remembers with glee how it all evolved.

* * * * *

She was sitting in her wing-backed chair by the patio door having her evening glass of chardonnay and swung around after hearing a tap on the screen. There was Barbara standing at the door. She was wearing cutoff denim shorts and a halter top. Both of which managed to reveal much of Barbara's salacious figure. Peering through the screen at Isabelle, she kept tossing her head and swishing her long auburn pony tail around as she spoke.

"Would you like to have some bricks?"

"Oh, hello, Barbara, come on in. Would you like to join me in a glass of wine?"

Barbara peered at her through overly long bangs. "I can't stay, but I came over to ask you if you would like some bricks?"

"Why on earth would I want bricks?"

"I thought I'd offer them to you. Have you seen our patio?"

Upon hearing this news item, Isabelle suddenly rose from her chair and peered across the way. She shrieked, "You've added twenty feet of brick work to your patio! For heaven's sake, did the board sanction this?"

"Oh, no, we just went ahead and did it. Isn't it cool?"

"No, it's not cool. You've extended your patio within a few feet of mine. I'm sure the neighbors and the board won't think it's cool." She frowns, saying, "It doesn't blend in and extends out into our community meadow. We all love the natural setting and spaciousness of the meadow. You've ruined it!"

"Listen, lady, don't get uppity with me. I was being neighborly by coming over to offer you these bricks."

"Oh, please. You just wanted to dump those extra bricks on me. You weren't being neighborly and the extension of the patio isn't a neighborly gesture either. You've got to be kidding with this neighborly bit."

"You know, you're not a nice person. In fact, you're a bitch. I'm leaving." With a swish of her hair and of her tail, Barbara disappeared.

Isabelle raced for the phone and dialed George Allen, the board president. "George, hello, this is Isabelle Weir."

"Well, the delightful Isabelle, how are you? I enjoyed your wine tasting the other evening. Great neighborhood get-together. What can I do for you?"

"George, I'm not delightful, I'm apoplectic. I'm calling to report a terrible infraction. The neighbors across the way have broken a covenant. They've just extended their patio out into the meadow. It's so ghastly looking."

"Here we go again," George sighs, "I don't know why folks don't read those covenants. It would save us a lot of problem solving. I'll have Doug take a look at it first thing on Monday. Which neighbors are these?'

"The people who live directly across from me. He's stationed in Korea and she lives here and has dreadfully aggressive tendencies. Can you imagine, she's always citing rules to the other homeowners and breaking them herself. You know some of these enlisted military folks; there are a few who think they can do anything when they're off base. They can be so pushy."

"Now, Isabelle, we don't want to create any trouble for our homeowners in the armed forces. You know that wouldn't look right. We've got to be careful here."

"Oh, bosh, George, she's broken the rules."

"Well, I'll see what the board can come up with."

"I'd be very grateful if you would move ahead on it." She purred, "In the meantime, you must come over for a glass of wine some evening."

"That sounds rather nice, Isabelle. I might take you up on that. But listen, you just keep your powder dry and stay out of trouble over there, let the board handle this matter."

"I'll be a good girl, George, I promise."

As she hung up, Isabelle began to dwell on Barbara and her past sins. Their patio resembled a Tennessee holler; Barbara had so much clutter on it. One architectural disaster was a faux-marble fountain with a cupid spouting water from his little thing-a-ding-ding, which actually wasn't little. This impish atrocity could all have appeared in a villa in Tuscany or, better yet, in the front of a Mafia household in the Bronx. Much to Isabelle's satisfaction it froze up during the first cold spell. Anyone who would attempt to install a fountain on their private patio in Colorado had to be certified partially insane.

To add to all of this nonsense this past summer, Barbara had fashioned a twelve foot wooden handmade trellis for raising grapes in their residential area. No one had ever considered growing grapes in the Broadmoor area. What would happen next? Isabelle remembered the year before that there had been a pumpkin patch. She began to fester thinking of all of Barbara's so-called enhancements. Because they were such an eyesore, these creative efforts were lowering the value of the neighborhood properties. And too, Barbara's personal appearance was a little bit "out-there." She watered her plants in her extremely revealing thong. Some of the men in the neighborhood stood by in a small communal crowd and marveled at her buttocks, which were the size of huge Crenshaw melons.

After much footwork and using all her persuasive powers, Isabelle persevered and the board saw to it the patio was returned to its original size. When Barbara's husband, Dick, returned from active duty in Korea and learned of the board's ruling, he made his thoughts known at the annual homeowners' meeting. He stated in no uncertain terms they were being discriminated against. On what basis discrimination entered into the picture no one could quite understand. His dialogue for standing up for himself caused quite a to-do. At the annual meeting, "fuck you" this and "fuck you" that reverberated off the ceiling of the A-frame club house. This caused much consternation on the part of the little old lady homeowners, who fidgeted nervously and, believe it or not, actually fanned themselves with their copies of the homeowners' budget. Many swore they would never appear at such an uncivilized homeowners' meeting again. Of course, Isabelle thought it was the best meeting she had ever attended.

"Meredy, please don't leave. It's just beginning to heat up."

"I'm not going to stay and listen to this disgraceful language."

Isabelle mouthed silently to George, who just happened to be looking in her direction to gauge her reaction, saying, "Stop him from talking before everyone leaves."

George shifted around in his chair and ignored her facial admonitions. He appeared to be transfixed by the drama of the occasion.

"Meredy, you're going to be sorry you left early. This can turn into a real wingding."

"Yes, Isabelle, and someone can get hurt. You stay and watch. You know, you have such an irreverent side to you. Sometimes I don't know why we're friends."

Sid, a neighbor sitting next to Isabelle, whispered that the property manager and men on the board were glad the verbal ranting continued. If that was all that was going to happen they were relieved. Dick was twice their size and Sid had mentioned to Isabelle they were prepared for a physical confrontation.

Fortunately, a few months later, Dick was deployed to

Iraq and everyone heaved a sigh of relief. The gardeners were assigned to take up the bricks from the expanded patio, which they finally did one day while Barbara was away.

As her thoughts return to the present, Isabelle decides to amble down to her book-lined den where she writes. Sometimes she is successful in adding to her collection of short stories, but often she simply surfs the net or plays solitaire. She isn't too happy with her somewhat desultory life lately. Since she has been laid off as a paralegal at the sheriff's office, she has been at loose ends. All this free time and what to do? You'd think she would be euphoric realizing all she had to do now was write. Writers call it unstructured time. It can be very troublesome. You have all these uninterrupted moments to produce something, so you put off the actual writing. Without competing activities and deadlines, she becomes lost in inertia. But outwardly she pretends all is well. At cocktail parties when folks inquire how her writing is going she responds, "Famously, just finished four more stories," and then takes a sip of her wine and dives into the brie. With her mouth filled with hors d'oeuvres, she gestures she can't speak further; that seems to satisfy all interested parties.

Suddenly she discovers the day has disappeared. She'd better hustle. This evening there is going to be a huge soiree up on the hill in tony Broadmoor Bluffs. She doesn't know how she garnered an invitation. She surmises the hostess thinks she is interesting and eccentric because she is a writer. With that in mind she selects attire to fit the hostess's perception. She digs out an old couture Schapperelli shawl, which her sister-in-law handed down to her and wraps it around her basic black linen. The shawl is so colorful and festive, embossed with subtle gold metallic threading. It reminds her of what the duennas might wear to mass in Spain. The gold will set off the blonde streaks in her hair. Sometimes being the poor relation in the family can really pay off. She's set the stage as far as eccentricity is concerned.

Isabelle races her second hand Volvo up the hill and nimbly parks in a surprisingly convenient and available space. As she walks up the winding drive, she looks back and discovers there's a fire hydrant at the rear of her car. How did that get there? Oh bother, she thinks, but continues making her way up the hill. As she makes her entrance, she notices she has drawn the attention of some who seem to be considering her unique attire. She smiles to herself. They appear to be attempting to get a take on her. She doesn't reflect Gwen's usual guests. She chooses to ignore them, although she would love to take them on with a quip, such as, "A matador gave me this shawl after he killed a bull." But that might be a bit much.

She acclimates herself by studying the flowers and décor. The usual tall bouquet of calla lilies in a huge glass vase are placed upon a round marble-topped entrance table. She wishes hostesses would get off this calla lily kick, it always reminded her of funeral homes. She spies the open bar set up down at the end of the wide hallway. It appears they have two bartenders in attendance. It's going to be quite a festive party. There is a profusion of hors d'oeuvres set up on the glass-topped tables out on the patio. The Bountiful Basket must be catering. As she makes her way through all this extravagance, she hopes she won't have to suffer the usual Broadmoor dialogue this evening. She wants to concentrate on getting new story ideas as she observes all the party's participants. Sometimes dealing with the mundane topics brought up by her female acquaintances sets her teeth on edge. The conversations usually focus upon spending. The more they talk about spending, the more they elevate their self-esteem. Oh my, here we go. Tiny, svelte Serena Russell appears to be making her way across the room in her direction. What in God's name is she wearing? She looks as if she's just come down from yodeling in the Italian Alps.

"Isabelle, how have you been? I believe I haven't seen you in at least a year?"

"I know, Serena, I've been isolating myself in order to write."

"Oh, yes, how precious. Well, we've just returned from a summer in Provence. What do you think of my rural French provincial dress?"

Isabelle attempts to avoid the question, "Oh, I'd love to hear about your trip and make a comment about your festive attire. But instead wouldn't you like to have me regale you with my simple trip to Cheyenne Canyon for a hike on the Columbine Trail?" She shakes her head, saying "No, you go first."

Serena looks at her uncertainly and backs away a bit. Isabelle smiles. After these types of women begin to brag about their trips and purchases of couture clothing, they just never know how to take her quips. She focuses on Serena to see how she is handling her smart-ass comment, but Serena has apparently disappeared.

Isabelle edges into the quiet book-lined library as a respite. There appear to be only two other couples chatting amiably, so the room serves as an oasis from all the party-hype. She scans the titles of the books on the wall-length library shelves. Gracious, all the old classics. I didn't know Gwen and John were that well read. John's in venture capital and his conversation constantly centers upon "let's make a deal," so Isabelle's interest is piqued by this show of literary treasures. She spies the Booker prize winners lined up year by year. They don't appear to be re-arranged. They are in perfect chronological order. She pulls out John Banville's *The Sea*, the 2005 Man Booker Prize winner. As she leafs through, she has trouble opening some of the pages. They haven't been slit, which means they haven't been read! Who would have such a magnificent library and not read a book in it? She begins to check the leather-bound classics.

"Hello, Isabelle Weir, are you enjoying our magnificent library?"

Isabelle looks up, and smiles, "Hi, Gwen. Yes, I certainly am. You're so blessed to have all these treasures."

Gwen gives her an all-encompassing hug, "Oh Isabelle, John and I love to have folks enjoy our bounty. Please feel free to borrow whatever. We'd feel privileged to have you read them. As you know I'm not that literary."

"I'm not so sure I'd go along with that."

Isabelle smiles up at Gwen thinking some of her comments at a recent book group session were rather astute. What has made her so unsure of herself? Perhaps it's her inferiority about her hefty size, since Gwen looms almost two feet over her.

"Isabelle, I've invited you to the party because I thought you would enjoy it, but I also have another reason.

Isabelle braces herself.

Gwen continues, "John and I were having a talk the other morning in our cozy breakfast nook. We seem to have our best conversations at that time."

Probably so, thinks Isabelle, because, as she understands through the grapevine, John is usually plastered by two o'clock every day.

"He senses I might be suffering from a little bit of low self-esteem. He doesn't want his new colleagues to be aware of this. Their wives all seem to be so self-assured. He's come up with a brilliant idea. He feels if I write my memoirs I'll be more aware of my accomplishments and of course, so will others. Do you follow?"

Isabelle can only nod. She notices that as Gwen is engaged in conversation, she is shifting her posture drawing herself up to her proper size, rather than standing round shouldered and hunched over as she usually does in order to compensate for her height.

"So, I was thinking, well, knowing I am unable to write it myself, I was wondering if you might help me. John felt it might be better to leave it to you. Could you assist me with this project? He will pay you plenty."

"Gwen, what makes you think you can't write it?"

"Oh Isabelle, please, me write? How like you to encourage a friend. No, I couldn't possibly, and too, John doesn't want this to be an amateur endeavor. He wants it to have a certain polish. He feels it would be best if you would do it."

Isabelle stares at Gwen. Gwen has no clue why she has such low self-esteem. Everyone else knew at once upon meeting both Gwen and John. But perhaps after working with her on her memoirs, she might convince Gwen to look at herself in a new light.

After a long pause, Gwen breaks in, "I guess that look means no, doesn't it? John is really going to give it to me."

"No, Gwen, on the contrary, I was just considering how nice it would be to work with you. Yes, I'll accept your offer. It's called ghost writing and a lot of people do it. Please tell John I'm rather expensive though."

"I'm so glad you're willing to take me on. Now, of course, remember, as I said, cost is no issue. I have to see to my other guests, but I'll call you on Monday."

Somewhat non-plussed, Isabelle wanders into another room off the hallway. Her attention is drawn to the wall-length windows on the far side of the room. What a view! A scenic panorama of the early evening lights of Colorado Springs are twinkling on in the dusk, and then far off in the distance are the plains, reaching all the way to Kansas. The sense of well-being provided by this vista is interrupted by the conversation taking place between two of the party goers, immediately across the room. Oh my, there is portly, Jim Eads and tall, spindly Baxter Walpole at it again. She's remembers seeing them at the Golden Bee, the pub at the Broadmoor, animatedly involved in a heated debate. She draws closer to eavesdrop.

Baxter is leaning down and poking at Jim's chest, "They should nuke them, all the Iraqi insurgents. That's what they should do. They're murderers."

"Now, Baxter, take it easy. I consider them patriots.

They're simply protecting their tribal territory."

"You would take their side, you, treasonist!"

Lucy wondered if treasonist was a word.

Baxter continues, "I don't know why we have these discussions, Jim. You've never made any sense to me. What most of us know is, we should send all of Ft. Carson over there for hand-to-hand combat in Baghdad. Bush has the right idea."

"How many of those troops would we lose if we did that? You know that they are going to have to go house-to-house and you know what type of combat that is. The insurgents will pick them off. Some of the soldiers are over there on their third tour of duty? I can't imagine anyone having to serve under those conditions."

"They signed up. They read the small print in those military contracts."

"I doubt those kids even thought of reading the fine print on those contracts. Get real, Baxter. Do you know there's a brigade back East that has made a tour of duty six times? It's ludicrous, the sacrifice these young men have to make for the bungling of this war."

"I've heard enough from you with your lack of loyalty to our president. And I heard through the grapevine that you attended that secret meeting of disgruntled Republicans at the El Paso Club. You simpering idiots were unhappy because of the debt. You're disloyal and unpatriotic. I'm getting another drink!"

Jim looks over in her direction, she smiles consolingly as he shrugs and rolls his eyes. She leaves the room and joins the increasingly noisy party goers. What draws her sudden attention is Hatsy Toth lounging against the patio door frame in a rather seductive manner. She, too has somehow been able to isolate herself in this crowd-packed din, but for different reasons. There she stands at the edge of the room alone, appearing to be signaling with her body, "Hey, fellas, come and get me." Her cleavage in that bright red dress is remarkable. Isabelle has to hand her that. The signals seem to be working; gimlet-eyed Dave Bartram appears to be moving in her direction. Oh gosh, thinks Isabelle, I'm going to miss this dialogue.

She feels a gentle tap on her shoulder. Turning she finds herself staring into another pair of gimlet eyes. Lordy, lordy, she thinks. How do I deserve this?

"Well, hello, Herb. How's the world treating you this evening?" She'd try to be nice.

"Superino, Isabelle. I'm well into my book. Writing like a bandit. Got writer's bliss. It's really going well and sexy as hell."

"Oh Herb, aren't you the fortunate one to be so prolific and sexy at that same time. I guess it does all go together."

"Flattery will get you anywhere, Isabelle. But back to my book, I'm on the part where I'm stationed in Sri Lanka as a cultural attaché. The jungles are infested with all manner of poisonous beings and I'm writing about a few encounters with the nasty creatures. Plus there's a young nubile native girl after me."

"How fascinating."

"Do you want to hear about the part involving the insidious spider? It's quite uncommon, a rare species."

No, not really, thought Isabelle.

"The incident occurred at the end of our tour when we were stationed there. I'm not making any of this up, Isabelle. It happened."

"I'm sure it did. But I'm interested in how, you of all people, handled the brave, masterful stuff?"

Herb looks at her suspiciously. Did I go too far, she wonders. He appears to be collecting his thoughts, however, and continues as she helps herself to a huge portion of brie. She knows exactly what she is doing. Her eating disorder therapist has led her to believe her "eating over" occurs when she allows people to take advantage of her. She chooses to plow through the brie and give Herb affirming nods.

"Do you understand the gist of this part, Isabelle?" he queries.

She nods again. Why do men have to be such big deals? Here is Herb, telling her in this self-flattering manner how masterful he is with this dumb spider. She spies Penny, her dearest friend, making her way towards them. Oh, Penny, honey, thank you. You're coming to my rescue. Tawny-haired, evenly tanned Penny seems to be gliding across the crowded room effortlessly. She is wearing a slim beige linen shift with gold bangle bracelets and huge gold earrings as accessories.

"Hi, Izzy. Hi, Herb. I couldn't help noticing you both appear to be engaged in some scintillating conversation. My curiosity got the best of me."

"Herb is filling me in on the latest part of his memoir."

"Oh, Herb, dear, instead you should be focusing on Isabelle's writer's block. How unsolicitous of you."

"Well, I didn't know Isabelle had writer's block."

Of course not, Isabelle thinks.

"I developed it a few months ago, Herb. I thought I told you about it. It's downright frustrating."

"You'll best it, Izzy," reassures Penny.

They both turn to Herb. No solicitous comments

Isabelle continues, "They say writer's block is based on fear, but I don't know what I'm afraid of. Could it be the long isolated times one has to put in to be successful? Or am I afraid of being successful? Who knows?"

Isabelle senses Herb isn't listening.

Herb interjects, "Look ladies, I'm excusing myself from this conversation. I'm going over and help out Hatsy Toth. She seems to need my assistance. It appears she's sliding down that wall."

As he makes a beeline for Hatsy, Isabelle turns to Penny, "I owe you one, big time. Thanks for the rescue. Did you notice the minute I started talking about my writer's block, he lost interest in the conversation?"

"Oh, I don't know. Sometimes I pity the poor guy. He probably never got enough attention in his childhood and is demanding it now."

"Oh, bosh, you're being kind."

They study Herb and Hatsy across the room. Herb appears to be propping up Hatsy. Penny and Isabelle begin to giggle as they follow the repetition of the gestures across the way. As Hatsy slides down the wall, Herb attempts to get his arm under her fanny and hoist her up. This process repeats itself again and again. Isabelle and Penny follow the action in bemused amazement.

But when Hatsy begins to flay away at Herb, Penny cautions, "We'd better get over there."

"Oh no, I love just watching. Let's see what happens next."

"Izzy, you're incorrigible. Come on. Let's go over and rescue Hatsy, not that I'm so sure she deserves it."

"I don't know if that's what they want, Penny. Hatsy is intentionally standing there sending off signals. And Herb seems to be getting right into it."

"Yes, but Hatsy's attitude seems to have changed." Penny takes Isabelle's arm and leads the way.

As they draw close, Hatsy turns to them and appeals, "Get this ass away from me. He's trying to molest me!"

"Hatsy, I'm only trying to keep you from falling down on the floor. "

"You are not. You touched my ass, you ass. That's all you're interested in."

Isabelle giggles, saying, "This dialogue is so good."

Penny frowns, saying, "You know what, I think we all need some fresh air. Let's go out on the front veranda," she suggests.

She takes Hatsy's arm.

"Okay, but keep that ass from touching my ass!"

Isabelle giggles again as she and Herb dutifully follow. As they move outside, she notices the early summer evening air is chilly. That's good, perhaps it will chill off the presence of alcohol.

Hatsy warns, "Keep that pervert away from me," as Herb moves forward to seat her in an Adirondack chair.

"Hatsy, I am only trying to assist you in a gentlemanly manner."

"Oh please, you're not a gentleman. You're a lecherous over-bearing ass."

Herb draws menacingly closer, "Now just a minute, I'm getting tired of your innuendoes, you lush. You clam up."

After hearing this and spurred on by the alcohol, Hatsy rises up out of the chair and lunges at Herb, shoving him in the chest, pushing him across the porch with her fists. All of a sudden they've gone too far. Herb disappears over the porch railing.

Hatsy roars with laughter.

Penny shrieks.

Isabelle rushes forward and peers over the redwood railing.

"Izzy, is he all right?"

"I don't know Penny. He seems to be head first in the shrubbery. He's flaying about trying to upright himself. It must be a five-foot drop here. There, he's moved so he's standing, but weaving slightly."

"We'd better get Hatsy home. Are you sure he's moving?"

"I think so. He's attempting to claw his way out of the shrubbery."

As the three make their way to their cars, Isabelle glances back to check out Herb. She sees the shrubbery twitching. Must be good sign.

Later with all three women safely ensconced in their respective abodes, Isabelle sits alone on her patio in the moonlight. She has a huge candle burning on the patio table, so she can see to write properly. She is exhilarated. The evening's adventures have cured her writer's block. She's getting it all down on paper, gesture after gesture, along with the snippets of dialogue. I hope I haven't missed anything; Hatsy's smudged mascara, her spectacularly funny comment, "get this ass away from my ass," Herb's flushed face as he hoists Hatsy up the wall and then the final scene, his disappearance headfirst over the railing. What an exciting evening! Of course, first thing tomorrow morning when she's fresh, she'll embellish the story, but she won't have to do too much.

What's going on? What is that flashing light? It's shining directly into her eyes. The light appears to be coming from Barbara's bedroom. Lordy, lordy, could that witch be using a flashlight on her?

Isabelle chooses to ignore this aggravating distraction and continues to focus on the reworking of her writing. The candle is still burning brightly. She has more time.

What? There goes that flashing again. What is wrong with that woman? A few more details must be added to this story. After a while the flashing light ceases. Barbara must have gone to bed.

As Isabelle brings her work to completion, she experiences a strong sense of elation. What a wonderful day! She closes her eyes for a moment to rest. When she opens them, her gaze unconsciously falls upon the fire starter for the grill. The shiny tin can of liquid sparkles in the candlelight.

She rises, drawn to it. Wondering how much the tin contains, she unscrews the lid. There seems to be plenty. As if in a trance, she moves across her patio and in the direction of Barbara's huge ugly wooden trellises. As she silently makes her way across the lawn she tips the can, making a trail of shimmering liquid from the edge of her patio to the foot of the trellis. She pauses and gives a few extra squirts of fire starter to the base of the structure.

Returning to her patio, she brushes against the candlelit table. The lit candle and pens topple, tumbling on to the grass. Being a bit weary from all the evening's events, she enters her bedroom. Suddenly, she sees a stark flash of light flooding through her window. As she turns down the Provençal coverlet on her queen-sized bed, she smiles to herself. Accidents can happen.

Rising early the next morning, she can't wait to return to her writing. Her unconscious is unrelenting in its nagging to get the material stored in her head out and into the computer. She rushes to the kitchen to make her Columbian coffee. Grinding the coffee beans, she hears her phone ring. She pauses and listens to the message on the answering machine.

"Isabelle, it's me, Penny, you've got to call me right away. Something rather dreadful has happened to Herb."

Isabelle hesitates, thinking, oh, Penny, you're always overreacting. She chooses to ignore the call.

Coffee cup in hand and a sheath of papers in the other, she makes her way downstairs to her tiny book-lined study. Perhaps she'll put some Mozart into the tape deck. Yes, yes, Iona Brown and St. Martin in the Fields performing the Haffner. It's so triumphant. As she descends, she suddenly hears a great commotion outside; a shrill wailing across the meadow. Gracious, what a din. Could it be Barbara? Can't imagine why is she yelling like a banshee. Isabelle smiles benignly. Actually, she can imagine what might have set Barbara off. Perhaps she'll make it into another neighborhood story. What a wonderful day! Her long-term writer's block has finally subsided. There are so many good story ideas. She'll be busy all morning. Life is good.

Custer County, Colorado

Amanda Harrington

> "Under the West's water laws, claims are hierarchal. The oldest, first filed claims, many dating back to pioneer days, get water first, with newer claims at the bottom of the pecking order." —*New York Times,* April 4, 2007

Standing at the edge of the ditch and gazing down, she thinks damn fools; anyone can see what the problem is. Hearing a motor off in the distance, she looks up toward the direction of the sound. Her gaze searches the horizon, but no one seems to be approaching. As she shades her eyes to better see, her attention is drawn to the Colorado sky; cerulean blue with white, fluffy cumulus clouds reaching toward the heavens. Cattle are grazing on fresh green pasture. One of this season's calves is sprawled in the middle of the shallow part of the irrigation ditch, enjoying the water. Even though the picture of the calf relishing his bath in the rippling water offers a bucolic scene, she scoops him up and places him upon dry land, so he doesn't get a chill.

This is such a beautiful day, does it have to be spoiled by this worthless bunch? They are due to arrive about eleven thirty, midday, so they can better inspect the flume in the brightest sunlight. Developer, Keith Overman, and his project manager, Sanchez Green, have committed to this meeting. As she waits she ponders, will Sanchez be disrespectful to her again? Every time he comes on the property to measure the water diversion, he treats her with disdain. She understands his resentment over a gringo woman now owning the property his family was deeded in a land grant two hundred years ago. But *she* hadn't caused his family's loss of ancestral property. His frustration is becoming more and more intense. She's losing her patience with him. His outward show of animosity is beginning to frighten her.

The sound of an engine draws nearer. Finally she sees the huge Dodge truck clear the crest of the hill and come barreling down the gulch toward her. What fools! They're making deep ruts with those massive truck tires. The late spring flooding has coated the gulch with heavy mud. Why hadn't they walked in as she had? Didn't they have any respect for the land? Apparently not. And it *is* her land.

Within thirty yards of her, they gun the motor, then come to a jolting halt just inches from her angular six foot frame. She doesn't budge.

"Morning, Amanda."

"Morning, Keith."

"Mornin', Miz Amanda."

She didn't bother addressing Sanchez. Just a nod.

"I don't know what you guys are thinking, driving that huge truck down through the gulch with all that mud. Look at the ruts you've made in the terrain. They must be at least a half a foot deep."

"Now, Amanda, don't get yourself in a tizzy over tire ruts. There will be another flood and those ruts will wash out."

"Well if it doesn't, Keith, you're going to have Sanchez smooth them out with a shovel and that would take quite some time." She looks in Sanchez's direction. He just shakes his head and grins.

Keith responds, "Amanda, let's not argue about tire ruts. You've got a list of grievances against me a mile long, so don't add tire ruts to it."

He shakes his sandy-haired head in chagrin. Then he moves his compact sixty year old frame down the ditch, gingerly edging towards the gate he has placed on Amanda's property to allow his allotment of water to pass on to his property.

"You see that," she says."Look at that. That's what I'm complaining about. You're getting too much water. Your gate doesn't fit square to the ground."

Sanchez edges down into the ditch and joins Keith.

"Looks all right to me, boss."

She snorts, "No, here, let me show you." She scrambles down almost sending both of them sprawling as she reaches the bottom. "Look at this wide gap. You can even see the sun shining through. This is causing the flow of too much water to your properties."

"Amanda, I don't see what the hell you're talking about."

"Look right here, you dumb ass, too much water's rushing right under the gate."

Keith glares at her, saying, "Now look here, Amanda, there's no need to use profanity. I've always considered you to be a lady."

"Well, that ladylike stuff hasn't worked, has it?'

Sanchez edges off the side to the top of the ditch, grinning at them. He seems to be enjoying this. She can see his gold tooth at the center of his mouth, sparkling in the sunlight. She wants to smack that grin off his smart-ass face. At least he's not calling her "Goldilocks" today. He wouldn't dare do that in front of his boss. Turning, she wants to shake some sense into Keith. Instead, she takes his arm and guides him closer to the gate and nudges him down eye level to it.

"There now, you can see it. The rays of the sun are coming through there. That shows your gate isn't built as close to the earth as it should be. There's seepage under it. You must be able to see it."

"No, I'm not certain I can."

Could Keith have ordered Sanchez to remove the silt beneath the flume to allow too much water to flow through? And now he's pretending to be unaware of it? She continues to block him from rising.

"Look harder."

"No, I can't see it Amanda. Move off now, I'm done looking."

She hesitates for a moment. Keith rises. His face is tinged with red reflecting his anger.

He squares off, saying, "You have a rather forceful way of explaining water seepage."

She pauses before her response and thinks, well if you're so dumb, maybe that's the only way to make you figure out what's going on here. She'll have to work around him to accomplish what she wants. She says, "Okay, this is what I'm going to suggest. Since we don't agree on this seepage, you check this out with your water law attorney first and I'll do the same with mine.

We'll get a water engineer out here. We'll have an impartial unbiased opinion. You pay half and I pay half. Then we'll go from there."

"Now, Amanda, I don't think that's necessary."

"Okay, then I'll take you to court and have you pay all those attorney's fees and costs. Would that be a better solution?"

"No way."

"Well then, let's just try this. Maybe we'll come to an agreement after we get the engineer's opinion."

"Okay, we'll try it. I'm a reasonable man. I want this dispute settled as soon as possible. We've bickered enough. Word's getting around town about it. I don't want any disputes tarnishing the image of Westcliffe Development Company."

He offers his hand. She hesitates, then shakes.

As the two men climb into the truck, she overhears Keith direct Sanchez to use the path next to the ditch. She watches them ease along and then crest the hill out of sight. She spies a red-tailed hawk hovering over the path, probably looking for field mice. If those jerks use the truck too often around here, the field mice and red-tailed hawks will all disappear.

She begins her trek back to the ranch house following the path along the water ditch. Thank goodness it's there; the water. It's so reassuring to see the stream ebbing along in a steady even flow. This winter they've had considerable moisture here in the Wet Mountains, what with two early fall blizzards. She hopes there will be enough water to last through the summer. But she's got to stop Keith's Overman pilfering of the water she has.

As she draws closer to the ranch house, she considers how this situation has been eating at her lately. Maybe it's because she's a sixty year old, single woman running a ranch and feels powerless against these guys. Then, too, she is considered a newcomer in this community, having just lived here twenty years, so there are those who have varying degrees of trust in this supposed "newcomer." But she doesn't want to make too many waves. In this rural atmosphere folks are expected to try and get a long.

About a week ago, she sought Dave's counsel. She met her ex-husband for apple fritters at the Amish Bakery on Main Street. The marital acrimony had been transformed into an amicable friendship. Dave didn't own the property anymore. It had been in his family for many years after his folks bought it from Sanchez Green's family in a foreclosure. Two years ago, Dave gave it to her in the divorce settlement. Having been with him for twenty years and experienced the shoulder to shoulder, back-breaking work they had to endure in order to make a go of it, she was grateful it worked out as well as it had. She dearly missed him, though. Of course, there remains the ever-abiding presence of the third party, Angie, the young nymphet David had acquired. But that doesn't seem to bother Amanda now. She had the ranch. At least she had gotten something substantial out of the mess. The ranch was her baby and those jerks weren't going to mess around with what was hers.

"Amanda, my sweetheart, I'm glad you asked me to meet you here."

"Don't give me that sweetheart stuff, Dave, I don't

need that. I need your advice about the ranch."

Dave gazes at her apple fritter. She shoves it over to him.

"I'm losing water. Overman's taking more than his allotment. I'm suspicious of that guy. How do you think I should handle this?"

"Well I'd keep an eye out. Continue to keep watch on that flume. Does Sanchez Green, Overman's manager, check the measurements?"

"Yeah, he does, but you know what? I'm afraid of the guy. He's so surly. Every time I see him now, he makes a point of reminding me his ancestors owned the property and that it's rightfully his. He's always coming up too close to talk to me and intentionally brushes up against me."

"Amanda, do you still keep a pistol under the seat of the pickup?"

"Yes, I do, but I try not to use the pickup too often because it makes tire ruts."

"Use the pickup from now on and be sure you have that pistol. Keep an eye on the amount of water going through that flume too. And call me if you see anything suspicious." He eases up off of the stool. "That's my advice for now, I've got to go. Angie needs me to take her to the hair dresser up in Colorado Springs for what she calls a 'new do.' "

"We must do what's important in life, right Dave? Thanks for the advice."

He tries to give her a peck on her check, but she brushes him off.

Mixed Signals

* * * * *

As she trudges along the water ditch, she remembers when she first noticed the field of vibrant green lawn surrounding one of the faux ranches on the property adjacent to hers. Keith Overman had built six McRanches on the thirty acres running parallel to her property. He had assured the Westcliffe Town Planning Board there would be no problems over water usage. So she was shocked when she noticed the acre of unprecedented greenery. She couldn't figure it out. Kentucky bluegrass in a rural Colorado environment? Investigating Overman's flume the next day, she discovered someone had lifted the gate letting water gush out in the direction of his developed properties. She had slammed the gate shut and decided to keep an eye out for what was happening. Early each evening she hid in the cottonwoods a quarter of a mile away and watched. The soft cacophony of sounds of "chip-chip-chip" from the sparrows and "ooch-oo-oo" from the mourning doves kept her company as she endured the long waits. A few days later, using her binoculars, she spied Sanchez Green, making his way towards the flume and opening the gate. The next evening, when she saw Sanchez appear and open the gate again, she flew out of the cottonwoods with a shovel and made a mad dash for him. She appeared larger than life with her six foot figure charging down the hill. Even though he had a fat, squatty body, he flew. He eluded her, scampering through the scrub and then through the fence to the green lawns.

First thing, early the next morning, she called Westcliffe Land Development Company.

"Keith, this is Amanda Harrington."

"Good morning Amanda, what can I do for you?"

"Well, I don't know if you remember me, my ranch is next to the properties you recently developed. We met at the meetings of the Westcliffe Planning Commission when you presented your application."

"Oh yes, I remember you being there. You attended every meeting."

"Something rather strange occurred on my property yesterday. I don't know whether I should report it to the Sheriff's Department. I thought I should call you first."

"Oh?"

"Yes, I ran off a small Hispanic guy with my shovel. He appeared to be tampering with the gates at your flume."

"Oh, really."

"I had checked your flume a few days ago and noticed the gate was open, allowing water to go to your development. The water gauge indicated you were receiving an unusually large flow of water." She shifted the phone receiver and spoke more forcefully. "You must remember the amount of flow was set up in the decree by the courts. This tidal wave is way over the allotted amount your developed properties are to receive."

"Well, this is all very interesting."

"Yes, it certainly is. Do you know who the guy might be? It looks like your worker, Sanchez Green. I'm used to seeing him check the flume once a week in the daytime, but never sneaking around in the evening. Did you give him authorization to do that?"

"Of course not. I wouldn't authorize such a thing. I'll look into the matter and get back to you on it."

"You'd better do that."

"Pardon?"

"I said you'd better do that or I'll report it to the sheriff!"

"Good-bye, Amanda."

She remembered waiting a few days. Then, returning early one evening to the grove of cottonwoods. She spied him. She could see Sanchez furtively making his way towards the flume again. He opened the gate. She pounded the shovel into the dirt. They are continuing to steal my water.

She yelled out, "Next time, I'm bringing a rifle," as he sped off.

Returning to the ranch house, she considered making a call to Dave for his advice. No, she would handle this herself. The next morning Amanda made a call to the water law attorney who had help draw up the original allocation plan in the past.

"Sueanne, this is Amanda Harrington. Your water law firm handled some past water rights issues for my ex-husband and me. I'm running Happy Valley Ranch by myself now. Someone is stealing my water. You have all the copies of past documents and decrees dating back to 1952 and I wonder if you could counsel me about this latest fiasco?"

"Hello, Amanda, I remember you. You were so on top of the facts and figures. I'd be glad to help you out."

Sueanne sent a rather forceful letter to Westcliffe Land Development Company asserting the possibility of a lawsuit and an estimate of damages due to Amanda's loss of so many cubic feet of water per day.

As Amanda again waited in the grove over a two

week period, the problem seemed to have been solved. There was no Sanchez. She gratefully sent a check off to Sueanne, thinking this was money well spent.

But a few weeks later, her rage erupted again over what appeared to be a more devious method of stealing her water. She discovered more seepage around the gate. Those thieving idiots; did they think I was dumb enough not to notice? She headed back to the ranch house to call Sueanne.

Sueanne said she would send an e-mail to Overman's attorney and send a copy to Amanda. What Overman was doing was illegal according to the original agreement.

Dear John:

I have spoken at length with Mrs. Harrington about the problem at the gate diversion structures. Contrary to Keith Overman and Green's belief, Mrs. Harrington, who is educated as a civil engineer, is convinced the problems she and they are experiencing are due to the installation of the augmentation station. Water runs around it. Over the past few weeks, the water that belongs to Happy Valley is being washed down the stream without permission. My client, Mrs. Harrington, demands Mr. Overman have his structure fixed, so that it does not interfere with Happy Valley's diversions. Mrs. Harrington believes she has suffered damages in the form of lost water and land damage for which she will seek recompense if forced into court.

Sincerely yours,
Sueanne Wolcott, Attorney for Amanda Harrington

Amanda was pleased with Sueanne's e-mail and after she read it was somewhat reassured the problem would go away since the warning of a possible lawsuit had been strongly worded. But a few days later she was alarmed when she received a copy of Keith Overman's attorney's response.

Dear Sueanne:

I had an informal phone conversation with the Water Commissioner and the Assistant Water Commissioner for the Wet Mountains yesterday. Both are in unequivocal agreement that all leakage associated with the diversion box is the result of the uphill flow on Mrs. Harrington's portion of the ditch, which creates head pressure on the box itself and a resulting leak around the gate. The Assistant Water Commissioner, Bob Smiley, personally attested to the proper installation of the diversion box, having himself actually assisted in its installation.

I continue to work with my client, Mr. Overman, as to how the disagreements with Ms. Harrington might be resolved without costly litigation. In good faith, they are offering to use sandbags to plug up leakage which concerns Mrs. Harrington, (due to the negative grade of her ditch). There would be no cost to her for this good-will offer.

Sincerely,
John Stevenson
Attorney for Westcliffe Land Development Company

Amanda was enraged when she read the copy of Overman's attorney's e-mail. She stomped around on the front porch of the ranch house making so much noise the cattle in the south pasture looked up from their grazing and moved further away. She strode into her office and sent Sueanne her e-mail.

> *From: Amanda Harrington, Happy Valley Ranch*
> *To: Sueanne Wolcott, Wolcott and Perkins*
> *Date: June 25, 2007*
> *Subject: Flash Flood and meeting with Sanchez Green*
>
> *Dear Sueanne:*
>
> *Since I last spoke with you, there have been flash floods down here. I am hoping against hope that the Westcliffe Land Development Company offices have washed into the Arkansas River and floated away. I've had enough of those knuckle-brained idiots.*
>
> *I almost went crazy when I read they were trying to blame the upward thrust of the hill being the cause of the seepage. The gall! Don't you think it is amusing that Bob Smiley, who is Assistant Water Commissioner, thinks the flume is okay? He installed it. What else would he say!*
>
> *Will keep my appointment with Sanchez to sandbag the flume. I shall leave the gate to the ranch open, so he doesn't use cutters on it again as he has in the past, and hopefully he'll drive the truck with care and the mud will have dried up by then. What is it that these people don't understand about DAMAGE TO THE LAND? They're sure not stewards of the Earth, just users of the Earth.*
>
> *This whole matter with these jackasses, plus the flooding, made me sit in the kitchen yesterday evening and bawl like a baby.*
>
> *Thanks so much for all your help. It keeps me from getting so riled up.*
>
> *Amanda*

The Dodge truck crests the hill. It is idling slowly due to what she surmises is the weight of the heavy sandbags. Finally it draws up to the flume and backs in as close as possible. Sanchez jumps out of the open driver's side. He is wearing a shirt and tie. Why in the Sam hill is he wearing a shirt and tie? What's with him? Sandbagging is heavy duty work.

"Mornin,' Goldilocks."

"Morning, Sanchez. Can we eliminate the Goldilocks business today? I've asked you to quit using that term before. It's insulting. I want this sandbagging and measuring to go as smoothly as possible."

"Okay, Miz Harrington, and with that in mind I brought some beer and pork rinds to make this go nicer."

"Beer and pork rinds? You brought beer and pork rinds?"

"Yeah, it will help us to get along better."

She snorts, "You want to make a picnic out of this?"

"Sure, I even brought a blanket."

"You must be joking."

"Miz Harrington, there's no need to be insulting, there are plenty of women who would enjoy a picnic on a blanket with me."

"Well, I'm not one of them. We've got work to do."

He glares at her. "Sure Goldilocks," and taps a beer.

They work steadily, discussing the placement of the sandbags to better shore up the flume. Sanchez intermittently pops a beer and eats the pork rinds. The sun is edging higher in the sky making it unbearably hot. When he runs out of beer, he switches to a bottle of Tequila he has in the cab of the truck. He is becoming unsteady on his feet. He lurches toward Amanda several times. Each time, she pushes him away.

"Stop it. You're deliberately bumping up against me."

"I can't help it Goldilocks, these bags are heavy and throw me off balance." He grins.

"I don't care if you're off balance. Just don't get near me."

As the day moves on, she feels a growing sense of unease. In the past she had experienced these feelings of apprehension when alone with him, but not on this level. They are almost finished and ready to check the gauge.

He has drawn too close to her as they take the water measurement.

She says impatiently, "I'll check the gauge Sanchez. You stand off."

"Okay, Goldilocks, you can do my job," as he staggers further down into the ditch.

He has never been drinking like this before. Loosening his tie, he begins to grin at her menacingly. She wonders if she should leave, but why should she? They are almost done. She'll move up to the top of the ditch.

"Looks like we're finished, Sanchez. The bagging seems to be blocking the seepage."

"Sure, Goldilocks, whatever you say. Sure Goldilocks, sure, Goldilocks, sure Goldilocks," he sings tauntingly as he lurches up the ditch towards her.

Her nerves are so on edge. With temper fraying, she warns, "Stay away from me. I told you never to call me that again. Maybe this will knock some sense into you."

She grabs the shovel and swings it toward him, hoping to hit him in the ass. He looks up just in time and throws up his arm to deflect the blow, but stumbles, losing his balance. He falls, his head hitting the edge of the steel flume. His body lies inert. He doesn't move.

"Sanchez, Sanchez?"

He does not answer. Scrambling down the ditch, she turns him over. Blood is gushing out of his nostrils, mouth and ears. She feels his chest. No pounding. She feels for a pulse. There is none.

What should she do? Reaching for her cell, she dials, "Is this 9-1-1?"

"Yes, ma'am, what is the emergency?"

"There's been an accident. He fell."

"Ma'am what are the nature of the injuries?"

"Yes, someone has had an accident."

"Ma'am, describe the injuries."

"Bleeding from the mouth, nostrils and ears. There's no pulse."

"Ma'am, the paramedics are in their truck, where are you located?"

"The Happy Valley Ranch off of County Road 141. We're just opposite the old Willow Schoolhouse. They'll see the ditch where we are, as soon as they enter the property. The road runs along it."

"Thanks ma'am, they're on their way."

There isn't a sound. Everything stands motionless. The sun is so hot and appears to be simply sitting in one place in the sky; even the hawks, mourning doves and sparrows have ceased their activity and have sought shelter from the heat. She checks for a heartbeat again. This waiting is unbearable. She checks her watch. Where are they? Why aren't they here yet? Should she call again?

She sees the reflection of a flashing light. There is no siren, thank God. No need to draw the neighboring ranchers' attention. The huge red paramedic truck bounds speedily along the path. She rises as it reaches them. There is a huge flurry of activity; doors slam, medical equipment hauled out, two paramedics bending over Sanchez. She edges away a bit. The young paramedics perform their tasks with efficiency.

"No pulse."

"No."

"No heartbeat."

"No."

They rise. One of the paramedics moves toward her, "John Riley, Mrs. Harrington."

"How do you do."

"I'm afraid there's nothing we can do. I'm sorry to say, he's gone. Was he one of your workers?"

"No, he wasn't. He was associated with Westcliffe Land Development Company. He was helping me sandbag the flume."

"Could you tell me how this happened?"

"He stumbled . . . ." She pauses.

"Was he drinking, Mrs. Harrington? There seem to be quite a few empty beer cans and over there next to the flume is a smashed bottle of Tequila."

"Yes, he was drinking." She looks John Riley steadily in the eye, but then begins to tremor. Her whole body seems to be giving out on her. Her shaking becomes progressively worse as they stand there.

"Mrs. Harrington, take it easy, you are experiencing shock. We don't want two fatalities in one day. We'll drop you off at your ranch house on the way out, but I want you to call your doctor and tell him about your tremors and what's happened. I'll write up my report with what you've just told me and what we've observed."

She overhears the other paramedic reporting to the dispatcher. After some discussion, both young men fill out their paperwork. They place Sanchez's body in a black vinyl case and then put it on a stretcher easing it into the back of the truck.

She rides in the cab wedged in between the two young burly paramedics. Their youth, competence, and strength inexplicably unnerve her. She begins to weep quietly. They arrive at the door of the white stucco, red-tiled ranch house.

"Mrs. Harrington, remember, call your doctor. Do you have any kin or friends who can be with you?"

"Yes, I do, thank you. Thank you for everything."

She enters the ranch house and for a moment leans against the huge solid oak door in order to gather strength. She heads toward the liquor cabinet, pouring herself a tumbler of bourbon. As she sits at her mother's antique pine table, she stares out the window at the sun setting in the west. It is comforting sitting there at that table gazing out at the darkening range. It is cool in the old ranch house. Over sixty years ago, it was built in this stand of cottonwoods in order to take advantage of their shade.

She chooses to call no one, keeping her own counsel. All she does is check the stock to see that they're well watered and fed. She waits a few days. She listens for the phone. The waiting becomes unnerving. Eventually her vigil of sitting at the comforting old pine table is interrupted by only one phone call, thankfully from Dave, who had evidently heard the news in town.

"Hi Amanda, I heard what happened and thought I'd better call."

"Hi, Dave."

"It's too bad Sanchez Green had that accident out there. Folks in town say he has been drinking heavily lately. Are you all right?"

"I'm perfectly fine, Dave. Almost over the shock. He stumbled and had a bad fall."

"Yes, that's what they said."

"Oh, to whom did you speak?'

"The paramedics."

"Such nice boys."

"Do you want me to come out and be with you? Check the flume where it happened? Or help you with the chores?"

"No, at a time like this you know, I like to be alone. And doing the chores takes my mind off everything. Did the paramedics say anything else? I'm wondering why the sheriff hasn't turned up here."

"The paramedics reported it as an accident and the autopsy and other reports verify that. There'd by no reason for the sheriff to show, Amanda."

Well, thanks for calling Dave, I'll call you later in the week."

"Just let me know, I'll be there."

As she settles down into the comfort of a rocker, she considers, what could she have done to prevent this? A death on my ranch! This is real trouble. Was she too forceful? Folks tell her again and again, she has that tendency. Should she simply have just walked away? But, Sanchez was baiting her. Did she have to respond the way she did?

Through the week, she continues to wait for a visit by

one of the sheriff's deputies. Or receive a call from the coroner. Or at least hear from Keith Overman. But there is nothing. Strange no followup, no questioning, no paperwork. But, perhaps it isn't strange.

He was drinking.

He did just stumble.

She shifts over to the chair by the pine table and sits by the wide window with its view of the eastern mountains. With the change in scene, she begins to consider a change in her attitude. Perhaps softening a bit. No, she's got to be tough. But look what's happened because of her toughness. Yes, if she gets out of this, she'll try to soften a bit. Not be such a smart-ass. She won't rush into action any more. She'll think first. Not react.

The Sierra Majodes loom peacefully over the valley. There are still vestiges of some snow on the top of the range even though it is June. The grandeur of those mountains has always been a source of strength to her. Now, at this moment, even more so. Those rough crevices have adjusted to climate change and the ravages of time. They have adapted and endured for centuries in this rural southern Colorado setting. She will follow their example and do the same.

Isabelle and Amanda

"I've got to get out of town, Amanda."

"I don't know if the timing is right with all that's going on down here right now, Izzy."

"Dearheart, what could possibly be happening on your bucolic ranch? Hoof and mouth disease?"

"Listen, Isabelle, someone died on my property just a few weeks ago. It was really scary. I was right there when it happened."

"Oh, no."

"Oh, yes. It's been rather dreadful. And I've been holed up here on the ranch with no one to talk to. Only Dave, my ex, called. I don't dare go into town. Too many questions."

"All the more reason why I should come down and visit. You sound depressed. I'll cheer you up."

"I don't know. I just don't know."

"Come on, Amanda, what are friends for anyway? We're both going through a rough patch. We'll lift each other up. Remember how we use to help each other out of the messes we got into at boarding school at Emma Willard."

"Okay, Izzy, I do love being with you. We always have so much fantastic fun. But no highfalutin activities. I'm not in the mood and certainly don't want to draw attention. And you always have a way of attracting attention. On second thought, I've changed my mind. Forget it."

"Listen to you. Highfalutin! What a word choice. To think you went to a private eastern school."

Amanda giggles. "I guess the Wild West has really taken over."

"Now, I know I've got to get down there to see you and instill some of that eastern culture we shared at Emma Willard. You're going to the dogs."

"Okay, I give up, but remember I want to keep a low profile. When Izzy?"

"Oh goodie, I'll start down at nine tomorrow morning. I'll go out this afternoon and pick up some of your favorite Michelle's chocolates and bring them with me."

"You're always so thoughtful. I'll see you tomorrow. Oh, I forgot. If you see a strange man in one of the pastures when you pull up the dirt road to the ranch, don't be surprised. I have a ranch foreman now, a cowboy. Dave talked me into it. He didn't want me out here all by myself any more."

"A cowboy, my, my, my. He'll be my box of chocolates, Amanda."

"No he won't. Don't you get any ideas, Izzy."

"Okay, I get the picture. I can't wait to see you and hear all about your troubles. It does sound serious, Mandy. I hope I can help you in some way. See you tomorrow and thanks ever so much for having me.

* * * * *

Isabelle makes good time down Highway 115. She waits until the commuter traffic at Fort Carson is out of the

Isabelle and Amanda

way before she begins her two hour trip from Colorado Springs to Westcliffe. That way she avoids being tied up by that beastly military gridlock.

As she speeds along the two lane highway in her antiquated Volvo, her thoughts turn to Amanda. How dreadful to have someone die on your property. She hopes it isn't anyone Amanda was close to. And now there is this mysterious cowboy. How intriguing! She can't wait to check him out. At least all of Amanda's news seems to have erased her own problems. The further she travels down the road, the more and more the events of past few days disappear. As she hurtles along, her memories of inadvertently burning down the neighbors' trellis across the way from her place seem to dissipate. And, then too, thoughts about the news of her friend, Herb, having contracted pneumonia and ending up in the hospital, after they had left him dangling from a hedge at a Broadmoor home during a cocktail party, have receded into the background. But now as she barrels along, she forces herself to remember that night. She is searching her mind to figure out if it really was that chilly out on the porch at that time. She imagines it must have grown much cooler later in that evening. Oh well, forget it. At least Herb hadn't died.

She makes a left at the light in Florence and promises herself she will forget all those pesky problems in Colorado Springs and simply enjoy her dear friend, Amanda, and her ranch. Passing by the federal prison, Super-Max, her thoughts shift to the inmates housed in that huge facility. Poor souls; she has been told their cells are all underground. They never see the light of day. She wonders how they can stand being imprisoned twenty three hours a day in a cell with no daylight. All the nationally known top criminals are housed there. Ted Kaczynski, the Unabomber, and the most dangerous of the Muslim terrorists. Even Bin Laden's secretary is incarcerated within those depths. Speeding along she thinks, well, we are all incarcerated in some way or other. How many of us have a true sense of freedom? She wishes she could escape her own quirky personality. Her desire for excitement always seems to get her in trouble. That's her prison. But at least, she can try to find a way out. Those poor devils incarcerated in Super-Max can't.

Her thoughts shift to the landscape as she races ahead toward ranch country. Custer County is partly rural farmland. It is mid-August and the ranchers are out mowing hay. Must be the second crop of the season. It is such a beautiful scene. Perhaps she should move closer to Amanda and get away from the suburbs. She feels submerged in the sameness of her surroundings and her friends. But what could she write about down here? Nothing ever seems to happen. It is all so wholesome and boring.

Out of habit, she slows as she emerges out of the national forest and moves into town. Thank goodness there are no hay trucks on the road. She shifts down to a crawl as she drives east through Westcliffe. There is only one stop light with no one waiting. How quaint. With a population of just 700, there isn't any traffic. In fact, there isn't a car in sight. As she waits at the light, she gazes at the Sierra Majodes, which rise sharply into the clear blue sky. The ranches at the edge of the foothills of the mountain chain are like a scene from a Remington painting. They all are beautifully kept and maintained. There are no vestiges of aging old farm equipment or cast off old cars. She supposes it's because the German population dating back to the beginning of the valley has set the standards. Or perhaps it's the Amish influence.

Edging through the sleepy town, she spies the red-tiled rooftop of Amanda's ranch house two miles away. She notices the verdant pastures reflect darkening shadows as the deep fluffy clouds pass over them. Isabelle passes by the charming, white clapboard one-room Old Willow School House built in the late 1800s. As she nears Amanda's dirt road, approaching from the other direction is the familiar huge Dodge truck, but with someone else, not Amanda, driving. It must be the cowboy; he tips his hat as she moves by. Her Volvo swerves as she attempts to get a better look at him. Oh my, my, my.

Making her way on to the rutted dirt road, Isabelle notices the ditches are brimming with water. It's a good sign. At least Amanda doesn't have water problems this summer. She approaches the sprawling white stucco ranch house, which because of the heat of the day looks extremely inviting as it sits in the shelter of the surrounding shade of the cottonwoods.

She cuts the motor. A figure comes racing out to greet her. There is her dear friend from boarding school rushing to her car. Amanda still looks so trim and attractive with her sun-bleached, blonde hair. She is wearing jeans, slimly cut and a red and blue tattersall shirt with a bandana at her neck. On her well-shod feet are good leather boots, of course.

They rush to hug each other.

"Hi, Izzy."

"Mandy, I'm so glad to see you. Thanks ever so much for having me.

"Well, you're welcome. You really made good time. No traffic, I gather. Come on in. I have lunch waiting. Then we'll go for a walk. I want you to see where it happened."

"What happened?"

Amanda stares.

"Where what happened?" she repeats. She finally gets it. "Oh yes, sorry. I forgot. The death. How obtuse of me."

"I haven't been back down there since and wanted someone to go with me for the first time."

"Oh sure, Amanda, I'll be glad to be with you."

Amanda smiles with relief.

"Let me help you unload your gear."

"What are we doing tonight? Are we going to the Westcliffe Inn? I always love that place with its historic charm, its cranberry hob-nailed glasses and pewter steak plates. And the food is always so good, especially the beef. It's about the only time I eat beef."

"The Westcliffe is closed for renovations. You'll have to settle for the Silver Peso."

"Oh dassit. I was so looking forward to the Westcliffe, but the Silver Paso sounds rather intriguing. What's it like?"

"Don't get your hopes up, Izzy, it's just a glorified western bar."

Isabelle and Amanda

* * * * *

They arrive at the Silver Paso at seven. Isabelle is wearing her beige silk shift and her arms are girded with fourteen-karat gold jewelry. Because of her high sense of style she cannot bring herself to dress in less formal attire. Out of habit, she feels compelled to "dress" for dinner. She has a light beige lace shawl over her shoulders. Amanda is wearing a long denim skirt with a white embroidered Spanish blouse and turquoise jewelry. They stride into the restaurant deliberately drawing attention to themselves by talking animatedly. Amanda wonders why when she's with Isabelle, do they have to make a grand entrance upon every occasion. Folks seem to be staring at Izzy. Amanda had felt it was useless to tell her to dress down.

Isabelle whispers to Amanda, "All of these women look the same. They have tightly permed hair are dressed in simple cotton shirt-waist dresses and wearing low heels." She grins, saying, "Their husbands are dressed similarly too, in true rancher style with bolo ties, clean white shirts, jeans and boots." She titters, "Why, some have even chosen not to remove their cowboy hats."

Amanda chooses not to respond, thinking it will only encourage Izzy to make more comments.

In spite of this Izzy continues, "They all appear to be having dessert. Does this town fold at seven o'clock?"

The heavy-set bartender approaches them and advises, "Just a few minutes ladies and we'll have a table ready for you."

"Thanks, Bill, no rush," replies Amanda. "Do you want to sit at the bar and have a drink while we're waiting, Izzy?"

"No, I'll just stand and enjoy this unobtrusive view of the natives. They're all so fascinating."

Amanda warns her, "Fascinating is not the descriptive word. Believe me, they are powerful. There is a lot of wealth from ranching in this small valley and the women are formidable. So be careful. I told you, I want to be low-key. There's been talk. This is my first time in town since the accident."

"The bar is beautiful. It simply gleams, it is so highly polished. It runs the length of the room doesn't it?"

"Back in the good old days in the 1880s this was a highly successful saloon. It was the era when silver was pouring out of these mountains. See that beveled mirror in back of the bar. That was shipped out from New York on a train with a flat car. Bill, the owner and bartender, has still retained some of the old accoutrements, like the gaslights, etc., but he put in two pool tables and a jukebox, which is a disgrace. They take away from the authenticity of the old western ambience of the place."

"Ladies, your table is ready," shouts Bill.

As Amanda makes her way, she quietly murmurs greetings to some of the locals, sensing she had better mind her manners. Isabelle follows, smiling and gently nodding. Amanda spies a friend and stops at her table.

"Countess, I would very much like to have you met my friend, Isabelle Weir, from Colorado Springs."

"How do you do, Isabelle, it is so nice to meet a friend of Amanda's. She's been a dear friend to me, especially during my convalescence. As you can see I'm still in a wheelchair," she sighs.

"Howdy, Countess," responds Isabelle.

Upon hearing this greeting, both women look at Isa-

Isabelle and Amanda

belle with astonishment. She shrugs.

The countess commences to introduce her hefty husband, Steve, who nods in greeting. She then turns to what appears to be a nurse, Lucibelle, dressed in a uniform. She also nods and then lowers her gaze ostensibly to study the tablecloth.

Amanda and Isabelle continue on following Bill to their table with a red-checkered cloth. They are placed directly in front of the huge fireplace, large enough for one to stand in.

Izzy remarks, "This isn't so bad, Amanda. We have a view of the entire room. My gracious, maybe I'll have a chance to meet some more of your neighbors."

"No, Izzy, I warned you, we are going to be very circumspect and not draw attention to ourselves."

"Okay. Listen, dinner is my treat, since you're offering me your hospitality for the week. Do you want to start off with martinis?"

A small tow-headed waiter draws near. Isabelle remarks, "My gosh, he looks just like the famous Truman Capote. That tiny elfin creature who wrote such beautiful prose.

"Good evening, ladies, what will you have?"

"We'd like two Stoli martinis on the rocks, young man, and would you please bring us a wine list. By the way, are you related to that famous writer, Truman Capote? He was a tiny elfin creature just like you. Perhaps you're a distant cousin?"

Amanda rolls her eyes.

"Ma'am?"

"Oh well, just bring the martinis and the wine list, dear boy."

After he rushes off, Amanda whispers fiercely, "Izzy, they don't have wine lists here."

"Oh Mandy, how do you know that, of course they do."

"This is just a western bar, they don't know what you're talking about when you mention wine lists. And bringing up Truman Capote is ridiculous. What has gotten into you? You should use more judgment."

Izzy smiles sublimely.

The martinis are placed before them. Isabelle says, "These look absolutely delicious. Thank you, now, that wine list?"

"Ma'am, I'll go ask, Bill, the bartender."

Amanda takes a hefty drink from her martini.

"Fill me in on the countess," Isabelle says. "She has such a sense of style. She is so attractively dressed, couture, I believe."

"Will you promise to keep this local gossip to yourself?"

"Of course," Izzy states, eyes gleaming.

Amanda looks at Izzy suspiciously, but starts in. "She left a count in Italy and took her rather sizable divorce settlement and invested it in a huge spread down south of town. She's absolutely lovely, gracious and charming and is the only one I seem to be able to socialize with in the valley." Amanda takes another sip of her martini, "Six months ago, Steve was driving her home from this place. He lost control of the car for some reason. Probably had too much booze. The countess ended up with a crushed pelvis."

Isabelle interrupts, "I got a hint of a suggestion of some silent goings on between husband, Steve, and nurse, Lucibelle. They appeared to be ogling each other secretly. If one can ogle secretly."

"That's not the least of it, Izzy. They are having an affair right under the countess's nose. But the countess is no dummy, believe me."

"Those two. No! Taking advantage of a wife in a wheelchair? What scum!"

Amanda grins, "Actually the whole community titters about it. Would you believe, Lucibelle teaches Sunday School and the moms are talking among themselves, saying she's a harlot. They want the pastor to discharge her from her church position." Amanda rolls her eyes. "But the countess is just waiting. I've heard from someone in authority in the local law firm that as soon as she's out of that wheelchair, she's going to dump both of them. So, there goes their meal ticket!"

"Way to go, Countess," giggles Izzy.

As Isabelle peruses the entrees on the menu, she asks, "What would you recommend, Amanda?"

"How about the buffalo burger? That would suit you just fine, knowing the aggressive mood you're in," says Amanda, smirking.

"Don't be peevish. Look they have meatloaf," Isabelle giggles delightedly. "I haven't had meatloaf in years. And it's served with mashed potatoes and succotash. We're back in the fifties! How quaint! I wonder what kind of cabernet would go with meatloaf?"

"How quaint? Are you spoofing this place, Isabelle?"

"A really good Louis Martini cabernet, that's what we'll have."

A group of bikers enters and makes its way across the

room to the pool tables. As they pass by they murmur, "Evening, ladies."

Isabelle offers them her best smile and says, "Good evening, gentlemen."

The waiter approaches and asks, "May I take your order?"

Isabelle blurts out loudly, "Young man, I demand you bring me a wine list, your service is lacking."

"Ma'am, we have a red we serve, and when we run out of that, we suggest the whites, like a chablis."

"Chablis. I've never met anyone who drinks chablis. Okay, this is what we'll do. Please go back to the bartender and ask him to write down the wines he has. I'll have another Stoli Martini. This is so frustrating, honestly, it's causing me to go over the edge. Do you want another, Amanda?" Amanda shakes her head.

Izzy looks up at the waiter, "We'll order two meat loaf dinners, please."

"Ma'am, I don't see any sense in having the bartender write the wines down. I just told you what we usually serve."

A biker yells over, "Do what the lady says, dude."

Isabelle smiles flirtatiously at the bike and says, "Thank you ever, so much. I just don't know why he can't comprehend a wine list."

"If you have any more trouble with him little lady, just give us the signal."

At that the ranchers, who are on their second cup of coffee look up and meet each others' eyes. Amanda notices the looks passing between them.

Isabelle smiles at the little leprechaun of a waiter returning with her second martini. "Did you manage to get the bartender to make us a list?

"Ma'am, he says all we have this evening is Gallo Hearty Burgundy."

"Oh, that couldn't be all you have in this establishment."

"Isabelle, shut up."

"Mandy, how can you speak to me that way?"

"Shut up."

"Hey, lady, your friend just wants to dine well," comments one of the bikers.

Another biker shouts, "Dude, go back to the bartender and get a list. Do what the lady wants before I shove this stick up your ass."

There is a scraping of chairs at all the adjoining tables. The ranchers rise in unison. Amanda senses real trouble. She is only too aware the valley has been waiting for something like this. There has been a lingering sense of tension lately. The natives have learned the taxes on their ranches are going to skyrocket due to wealthy, upscale weekenders from Denver, who have recently built vacation properties in the foohills of the surrounding mountains.

The bikers are shifting away from the pool table out into the center of the room.

A rancher speaks up. "What did you just say to our fine waiter here? He is top of his class in our local school and a member of 4-H."

"I don't care if he's Jesus Christ himself, he's to get these ladies a wine list."

"That's blasphemy. You shouldn't take the Lord's name in vain."

"Says who?"

"Says us."

Fists are clenching. Pool sticks are in hand. Beer bottles are within reach. Bill, the bartender reaches for the phone.

Amanda is so mad, she shrieks at Isabelle, "You've done it again. Tell them the list doesn't matter."

"But it does," smiles Isabelle appealingly.

A hefty rancher approaches her menacingly and begins to shake his finger at her. With that, a cue ball shoots across the room and smashes into his skull. He slips down into a chair, blood oozing from a large gash on his forehead.

As his wife dabs at the open wound with her napkin, she pleads, "Someone, call a doctor."

As if called to war, all the ranchers surge toward the bikers. As the thrust of ranchers nears, several bikers arm themselves with beer bottles.

Isabelle and Amanda sink in unison beneath their maple table, covered with the long, red-checkered cloth, thinking the cloth will place them out of sight and offer them protection from the ensuing danger.

As they hide under the table, Isabelle reminisces, "Oh, Amanda it's just like old times. Remember the exquisite fights in the bars along Nassau Street in Princeton."

Amanda grips Isabelle's arm and hisses at her, "You're responsible for this."

"*Moi*, poor, innocent *moi*? Don't be ridiculous."

And with that she reaches out under the table cloth and grabs at a snakeskin boot in order to trip up a rancher.

Amanda shudders. She thinks it belongs to Keith

Overman, an arch enemy who has been stealing her water.

Suddenly three shots are fired.

Silence.

The bar grows still.

Amanda peeks out from under the table and through the mayhem sees a young county sheriff with two deputies. All three look as if they are twelve and have only dealt with playground fracases.

The sheriff shouts, "Gentlemen, the party is over."

One of the deputies warns the customers, "If I were you, I would go home."

"Says who?" Keith Overman challenges.

"Well, Mr. Overman," responds the deputy sheriff, "That would be my choice. You see we've placed a call to Florence to be on standby. Those guys are retired from the Department of Corrections. As you know, they've dealt with hardened criminals and don't mess around. Of course, it's your choice."

With that the bikers are out of the Silver Peso in an instant, firing up their Harleys. Trembling wives push their staggering, wounded husbands towards the door. One wife gives the finger to Izzy, which provokes huge guffaws from the ranchers. Bill and the waiter begin to right chairs and tables. Bill shaking his head in consternation.

"It sure took you long enough, Riley."

"We came down the hill as fast as we could. It's well within a five minute response."

"In those five minutes, I'll wager there's been about five thousand dollars worth of damage and you didn't have to shot three holes in my 1890 tin ceiling." Bill turns to Isabelle and Amanda saying, "Ladies, I think you'd better go home. Until you walked in here everything was going smoothly."

"I beg your pardon, my good man, are you asking us to leave?

"Yes, ma'am, I am and with good cause."

"Well, the very idea . . ."

"Shut up, Izzy," hisses Amanda.

She shoves Isabelle towards the exit. But as they approach the wide doorway, Keith Overman appears to be blocking them. And what's more, Amanda notices, he has one boot on and one boot off.

"I don't know which of you has my cowboy boot, but it's missing and seems to have slipped off when I passed by your table during the fight."

Isabelle smiles up at him, reaches into her huge Louis Vuitton bag, pulls out the boot and teasingly hands it to him. His coloring shifts from ashen to a slowly emerging purple. He looks at her with disgust.

Amanda breaks in before he can express himself, "I'm terribly sorry, Keith, for the inconvenience."

"You'd better be sorry. Your trouble making is going to catch up to you real soon." He looks right through her.

As they emerge from the smoke-filled restaurant, the cool, damp, evening summer fog is moving into the valley. Covers of clouds hide the moon. It's so dark, Isabelle hopes she can manage the Volvo on the unfamiliar road back to the ranch.

Amanda pulls her denim jacket close about her shoulders and as she does, she glances back at the Silver Peso. She remarks to Izzy, "That's trouble. I see Keith speaking to someone on his cell phone.

Isabelle and Amanda

They climb into the Volvo and Isabelle eases out of the parking lot, down through town and out towards CR 141.

"Amanda, I'm sorry. I'm so sorry. I can see my hand in this."

Pasture land hurtles by as they speed along the county road.

"Please, talk to me, let's talk this out."

Amanda's face is rigid. She does not respond.

The moon slips out of its cloud cover and bathes the valley in light. Isabelle can smell the newly-mown hay. It is delicious. It is a beautiful evening. If only she hadn't ruined it. She wishes Amanda would talk to her, but Amanda appears to be glancing out the back window.

"We're being followed."

"What? How do you know?" queried Izzy.

"A truck has been tailing us for the past twenty minutes. I'm calling Ralph, my ranch hand, on my cell and telling him we're being followed." Amanda speaks, "Ralph, we're on our way home just going by Willow Glen School. Someone is tailing us." A moment passes. She clicks the cell closed. "He's coming."

"How do you know we're being followed? Aren't there a lot of pickups that use this road, after all it's one of the main roads through the valley."

With that, the huge black truck directly behind them pulls up close to their rear bumper and nudges it.

"It's going to be all right Izzy, hang tough."

The truck lights beam higher. It moves even closer.

"I can't see how close he is Mandy, his lights are so bright."

"It's okay Izzy, just move along as fast as you can."

The truck nudges the Volvo's back bumper again. One more time with more force.

Izzy tries to gain control of the car after that third hit, but swerves back and forth along the road, finally pitching off to the side into a water ditch. The truck roars past.

Izzy and Amanda aright themselves, attempting to tame their nerves.

"Are you okay?"

"Yeah, you?"

"Yes, I'm fine. I'm calling Ralph again. Damn, I can't reach him. He must have left the bunkhouse without his cell."

"Maybe that's the last we'll see of them, Amanda."

It is silent. They wait.

What to do next?

The huge black vehicle has done an about face. Suddenly it roars back down the road and pulls up facing them. It idles in place for a few minutes. Abruptly its rooftop lights flash on. Isabelle and Amanda are blinded. Two car doors open and slam shut.

"Izzy, lock your door."

Isabelle can make out two huge shapes on her side. The third is on Amanda's.

An attempt is made to jerk open the doors. Failing at that, the shapes begin to shove and rock the car. The figures laugh tauntingly. The car tilts back and forth from one side to another.

Izzy, hanging on to the door pull asks, "Will they tip us over?"

"They're sure trying to. Keep calm, Izzy. We need our

wits about us. Don't make any noise. Don't let them know we're scared," cautions Amanda.

From outside the Volvo, they hear, "I got the blonde."

"No, I got her."

"Don't fight about it, there's plenty there. First thing we're going to do is rip their clothes off. Put them in front of the lights. Then we'll each have a turn. Both of them, but the blonde first."

Izzy and Amanda hug each other in terror as the car tilts further to each side. It is almost ready to go over.

Suddenly, for whatever inexplicable reason, the figures dart off toward their truck. Its roof lights flash off as it speeds back down the road.

Clop, clop, clop.

Amanda laughs with nervous relief as she raises the window and hears the sounds of hoof beats.

"What, what?"

"The Amish. It's the Amish in their buggies."

The sound draws closer. The dim small exterior lights can be seen on the front of each of the two buggies.

"Whoa, whoa, there."

"Good evening ladies. Looks like you got yourselves into a bit of a fix," says a burly wholesome tow-headed teenager as he approaches the car.

"We were run off the road."

"Oh, sorry business, ma'm," responds the second teenager. "We saw someone come flying past us. Did you recognize them?"

Amanda responds, "No, but I have an idea who might have sent them."

"Well, we can't handle that, but we can sure lift this vehicle out of the ditch and get your car righted. We were on our way to town to help lift some flour sacks out of storage into the bakery. But that can wait."

"We'd be so grateful. Otherwise we're stuck here and I'm afraid those guys might come back"

It took no time. The teenagers dressed in overalls and sturdy boots had the Volvo up on the road facing the ranch in just a few minutes.

"We'd better see if that engine runs before we leave you."

Suddenly a dark figure appears out of the shadows of Amanda's pasture. The figure has a high-powered rifle pointed straight at them.

"No, Ralph," warns Amanda. "Put that gun down. They're helping us. They got us out of the ditch. Someone else ran us off the road."

"You sure?"

"Of course, I'm sure. Now put the gun down."

The teenagers back off and warily head toward the buggies continuing to eye the gun. They move quickly down the road.

Isabelle moans, "We didn't even get a chance to thank them."

"Well, let's get you both home. You must be really wiped out."

As Ralph pulls the Volvo onto the ranch road, Amanda announces, "Izzy, I'll be getting up early tomorrow morning to feed the stock, so I won't be able to say goodbye when you leave. So, good-bye."

Isabelle saves face with a disappointed, "Oh good-bye, Mandy, thanks for having me down." She reaches over and tries to hug her friend.

Isabelle and Amanda

Amanda pulls away, eying her sternly, and then says nothing. As they reach the ranchhouse, she strides over to the barn to check the stock.

* * * * *

The next morning as she arises, Isabelle ponders last evening. What is happening? First she was asked to leave the Silver Peso and then her dearest friend implied she'd better get off her ranch. This is outrageous, this can't be happening to her. Two rejections in one evening.

As she hears the front screen door to the ranch house slam, Isabelle surmises Amanda is on the way out to do the chores. No offer of coffee, no rehashing of the evening's events, and no gushy good-bye hugs. She gazes east towards the Sierra Majodes. There they sit in all their majesty. The sun is sliding over the range making its way across the valley. It's going to be a beautiful day. Ruefully she acknowledges, she is not going to be allowed to stay and enjoy it.

After dressing and making herself a cup of coffee, she lugs her gear out to her car. Full of regret she eases the Volvo down the ranch road. She waves to Ralph, who appears to be mending the fence they careened through last evening. He tips his hat. The cattle are grinding the moist grass near the ditch and then lapping up the water with their fat tongues. She savors the sight. Her regret returns. Somehow, she's blown it again.

Moving through town, she spies the Amish Bakery, pulls up, hops out of the car and enters to order a coffee for the trip. She asks for a favor from the calico-dressed young Amish woman behind the counter. Does she see the Amish kids in town? Could she pass on a donation to the three young boys, who helped them on that lonely road last evening? The young woman agrees to ask around and assures Isabelle she will give the sizable donation to the boys. As Izzy leaves the café, she is feeling better.

There's plenty of time to mull over last evening's events as she moves through the national forest on her way home. Why do I do it? Why do I create this ditsy, unneeded excitement? Yes, it can be fun and hilarious. But what if it hurts others? Look what I've done to Amanda. As Isabelle speeds by Super-Max she ponders, do I create this excitement because I'm in a prison of boredom? Isn't there another way of finding release from this particular confinement?

She reaches the red light at the corner in Florence and searches for her coffee as she waits for the light to change. As she looks through the pile of papers on the front seat, she spies the Michelle chocolate box. Apparently she hadn't given it to Amanda or perhaps Amanda had returned it to her out of spite.

Heading north towards home, her mood changes with each passing mile. Amanda will get over it. The town will settle down after all of this. A few months from now they will reminisce about it at the bar in the Silver Peso. She reaches inside the box and digs out one of the creamy white milk chocolates meant for her dear friend. She bites into it and savors the smooth, sweet taste. In the center is a macadamia nut. She pauses and experiences a moment of bliss as the rich chocolate slips down her throat. My, oh my, what chocolate does for a woman. She won't get herself in a dither about last evening's silly events. She bites into another chocolate as she speeds up Highway 115. Her sense of remorse has vanished.

Epilogue

The Things She Knit

She is a sturdy little girl with long blonde curls and bright blue eyes, typical of her Scandinavian heritage. At age ten her mother and grandmother teach her the craft of knitting. She sits on the edge of the durable corduroy sofa with her grandmother seated close by, guiding her hands, as she twists and turns the aluminum needles in and out of the bright red stitches. She adores sitting next to her grandmother, who always smells sweet and fresh because of the Lily of the Valley talcum powder she wears. Although she makes many mistakes in her attempts to master knitting, her grandmother appears not to notice.

Grandmother is her father's mother. Her father has disappeared. No one tells her where he has gone. Daddy is just no longer there; taking her to the beach to jump the waves, or reading the Sunday funnies to her, or pulling her and her brother in their red wagon, or taking them all for Sunday drives. She wonders sometimes if she's done something bad to chase him away? Was she so naughty?

She sees her paternal grandparents often. They are a constant presence. They take her to the rides at Asbury Park, a seaside town, every weekend. She and her brother visit them in their screened in house beside the ocean. When they sleep in cots on the screened-in sun porch at night, she can hear her Grandma and Grandpa talking into the morning hours. There is no laughter. Sometimes she can hear her Grandma crying.

Finally, at last, the red scarf she is working upon is completed. She wears it to school with her Scotch red-plaid jumper. Her grandparents are of Scotch descent and quite often her grandfather dons his clan's navy and dark green kilt when they walk the boardwalk on Sunday afternoons. He is very proud of his Scotch heritage and often speaks in a brogue she can barely understand. He reminds her that she too, belongs to the Graham Clan and to never forget it.

In high school, she knits argyll socks of many colors for her boyfriends. Her mother never complains about the cost of the many colors of yarn since it keeps her from pestering. She has learned not to bother her mother.

Her mother's responses of, "I am too busy, I have to be both a mother and a father to you, and your brother, Bobby," has taught her not to ask for help.

Her mother is of Swedish heritage and is quite strict—a Swedish Lutheran. There was a long tradition of knitting in Sweden. She remembers her mother knitting dozens and dozens of socks in a drab olive color for the young men who were in the trenches fighting World War II.

The argyll socks for her high school boyfriends are difficult to knit because of the many plastic bobbins, which hold the colorful yarns. Each bobbin has to be twisted around the next bobbin in order to make a color change and not create a hole. Because of this process the knitting of the socks is daunting. Inevitably she "breaks up" with the would-be owner of the socks, or he with her before they are completed. Adolescent love has a short time span. There are at least five single argyll socks stashed away in her pine bedroom dresser.

Upon finishing high school, she is put on the train, accompanied by only one trunk of clothes, to make the journey from her Jersey shore beach town to a small college in southern Ohio. She is worried about making the trip alone all by herself. But upon entering the train at Newark, New Jersey, she discovers many new classmates in the same train car. She remembers to wave good-bye to her mother, who is smiling at her through the train window. She attends the Methodist liberal arts university for four years and continues to knit argyll socks through her freshman year. In her sophomore year, she receives a fraternity pin. Upon becoming "pinned," she knits the "pinner" a beige V-necked lamb's wool sweater.

During the summer vacation of her sophomore year at her beach town on the Jersey shore, she experiences a new, unexpected encounter. At one of the many evening beach parties, she meets a fun-loving, outgoing sophomore from a Catholic university. He draws her attention with his gregarious manner. He is full of life while her nature is relatively shy. She has always had to behave and be quiet and has never been with someone who could engage in so much mischief. He comes from a wealthy family. Together, they attend a bevy of beach parties, formal black tie dances at his family's beach club and meet under the clock at the Biltmore in New York City. He is summer interning at his family's brokerage firm, so she knits him a pair of long dark, navy business socks. She writes a note to her college sweetheart returning his fraternity pin. Many years later, she regrets how she must have hurt her studious, quiet, college sweetheart.

The summer after she graduates, she marries the fun-loving guy. The wedding is considered the social event of the season. The New York Times posts her picture and a wedding announcement with a listing of his socially prominent relatives residing in Manhattan. She has converted to Catholicism in order to marry him. She patterns herself after her mother-in-law, who gives her much needed attention and guidance. She learns how to deal with the help, how to entertain properly, make no social gaffes, and how never to offend. She seems to giggle a lot and say trivial foolish non-offensive things. She wants to please. All too often there are times when she is swallowed up by social demands. There are occasions when a member of the family will search for her at the supper parties and tea dances. They will find her in the quiet shadows at the end of a long wide terrace all by herself. This just isn't done. Although she has many obligations, she turns to her knitting for relief. She knits her new husband brightly colored V-necked golf sweaters. And while she knits, she becomes aware of a growing sense of dissatisfaction as she works on the repetitive rows and rows of stitches. In trying to please so many, she's lost her self. She seems to have disappeared. She makes a decision to break away. She chooses to teach. Her major had been elementary education in college. It is the late fifties. Often it is frowned upon for women of her class to work, but young upper class women are beginning to come into their own She finds herself in a classroom filled with second grade children—second graders unstintingly adore their teachers. She gratefully loves them in return. Her confidence rises. She feels more at ease with herself.

Because of her growing assuredness, she finally faces up to the insurmountable marital problems. The family wants this matter hidden. A Jesuit priest counsels her and offers her comfort and guidance. She persists in her need to find answers and deal with the problem. There is resistance. Nothing could be wrong with a member of this family. They are above reproach. She begins to sense it is her fault. After all, it couldn't be his. The marriage is annulled. Later in retrospect, she takes pride in ending that unhappy marriage, but she also came to another realization. Had the family in its own careless manner simply discarded her? After a few years she chooses to move away. She climbs into her little VW and drives to San Francisco for a new start.

In her new setting away from family and friends, she attempts to get her footing. Because of some residue of lingering emotional turmoil, she can't seem to concentrate enough to knit. Attempting to find herself in a new setting and come to terms with her past seems very similar to encountering the "ninth wave." As kids growing up on the Jersey shore and swimming in the Atlantic, there were many limits. They were all warned after a hurricane not to go into the water. The tides were too turbulent. You might encounter the dreaded "ninth wave" and be dragged under. This is her "ninth wave" and she is desperately trying to get her bearings. It is the sixties in San Francisco, an exciting, experimental time.

Not the best of environments, however, for getting your emotional balance. Because she has to earn a living, she returns to the classroom and again a little group of second graders restores her sense of self-worth.

She seeks out many partners, trying to come to terms with her relationships with men. After two years, unexpectedly and without warning, her life takes a glowing turn. At Children's Hospital, in San Francisco, early one morning, she finds herself placing a soft, gauzy pink blanket she has hurriedly knit on the radiator by the window. She wants to warm it for her new baby, since the cool summer fog is shrouding the bay area.

Because of the necessity of caring for her new husband and dear baby girl, and also their new rustic summer cottage way up on a hill in Mill Valley north of the city, she finds little time to knit, but she is eventually able to find free moments to diligently work on a V-necked Shetland wool sweater for her new husband. She is so grateful he has taken them on.

A few years pass, the baby thrives and needs less care. She begins to knit gifts for everyone around her. Her knitting friends are amusing companions and very wealthy, since they live in affluent Marin County. They spend outrageous amounts on Missoni yarns from Italy, Hebrides yarns from Scotland and Peruvian alpaca. Eventually these same friends will offer loving support and solace. Her husband's re-emerging, self-destructive ways of the past are becoming a concern. Years of smoking and drinking have taken their physical toll. She had chosen not to give too much attention to his past, since he had been relatively problem free when they met, but

The Things She Knit

with the pressures of providing a livelihood for a family, his old negative tendencies had returned.

Finally the consequences of these oversights have a tragic outcome. On cool summer days after years of distress, she finds herself sitting alone in her living room next to the warm fire meant to burn off the chill of an early morning fog. She has chosen to return to her knitting as a source of comfort. The ivory lace shawl of cashmere and silk is very difficult. She cannot concentrate. With 186 stitches on her wooden needles and various knit togethers and yarnovers, she finds the project daunting. The weeping doesn't help. The tears flow on to the yarn and block her vision. How many tears does one shed? When does the pain go away? The shawl is finally completed and she enshrouds herself with it as she climbs into bed every evening. She reaches for his hand, but it is gone; he is buried in a not too distant cemetery.

She begins again. She knits career sweaters of gray and ivory, three quarter length to go over silk blouses with light weight skirts. It is a soft look compared to the power suits woman are choosing at the time. While knitting on the Larkspur Ferry as she commutes back and forth across the bay to her legal position in San Francisco, she observes that when she wears her soft look and knits, she attracts the attention of fellow male passengers. They will sit next to her as she knits and entertain with conversation.

"My mother knit most of her life."

"Oh really."

"Yep, she knit mittens for me to wear while skiing at Tahoe."

"That's so nice."

"You wouldn't be interested in coming over to my place and seeing if you can mend those mittens?"

"No I'm afraid not. Right now, I'm busy raising my teenage daughter. Maybe, sometime in the future when I have more time."

If she wears her navy striped power suit and reads the Wall Street Journal, she sits alone.

Her dear daughter graduates from the local prep school, Marin Academy, and then leaves for the University of California-Santa Barbara. She is alone. There are evenings and weekends of silence and loneliness. She does not knit. She drinks a lot of red wine, pretending she is a wine connoisseur, but that isn't the real reason. In retrospect, she discovers, wine was her companion.

She is finally saved from what she considers her comforting vice. One day, for some inexplicable reason, she is passing by her old haunt, the yarn shop in Mill Valley. What a waste, attending wine festivals and tastings. She could have indulged herself with two sticks and a piece of string. All this time she could have been knitting with a purpose. She peeks in the window and there are pinks and blues, lemons and limes in new yarns and brighter shades. She enters. Rummaging through the new brightly colored baby yarns, she notes this is the way it should be. Why have babies in old-fashioned dull, faded colors? The new color choices are vibrant. She chooses a knock-out bright blue.

Her old dear friend and the proprietress of the yarn shop, Connie, approaches her and greets her warmly.

"We've missed you."

"Well, thank you, Connie. I've been into other ventures."

"And now you're going to be a grandmother. How wonderful!"

"Oh no, Anne's just in her junior year at UC-Santa Barbara, not even married."

"This is for a niece then?"

"No, this is for me to work on. I'm going to begin."

"Begin what?"

"Just begin that's all."

"You're going to begin knitting for babies who don't exist?"

Yes, you've got it exactly. This is a smashing blue, don't you think?"

"I don't know about this, what if your daughter doesn't want children? This would be very unfair. She's going to see you knitting for an unborn child?"

"Just sell me this blue yarn, Connie, don't judge me."

She hides all the finished bonnets, booties, pram blankets under her bed and the guest room bed. No one knows what she is about.

Five years later, she receives a phone call from Colorado: a baby is coming. Her daughter and new husband had moved to Colorado Springs. She gazes out the window at the stately redwoods and eucalyptus. She savors the scent of bay leaves off her redwood deck. She thinks, I'm going to miss all of this. And my friends, my loving, knitting friends. When the movers arrive they quickly pack, all but the hand-knit garments placed in plastic bins on her kitchen counter. These precious items will be placed in the back of her station wagon; she will not trust them to movers.

As she drives from the San Francisco Bay area to the Colorado Rockies she looks forward to being surrounded by wee ones and new adventures. She remembers her pilgrimage to San Francisco and all the adventures and activities it offered; thirty years of building a life, a family, close friendships; the San Francisco Symphony and Opera, Napa Valley, Lake Tahoe, southern California, Santa Barbara, Del Mar. Although there had been many challenges, there was no regret.

She makes many visits to the parks with the wee ones. They take weekly trips to the libraries. At first she is besieged with the diaper changing, but then graduates to watching soccer and Little League games and listening and vigorously applauding at recitals. Her heart bursts with pride. She discovers the yarns shops on the Front Range are filled with sturdier patterns better suited for icy, cold outdoor life—wholesome durable worsteds for caps, mittens, scarves and such. The "knitting season" is very long. Sometimes one is socked in, in a blizzard with nothing to do but knit. Heaven!

Now she is seventy-three and coming to terms with the diminishing of years. She is reaching the season of winter in her life. There is not much time left. She is surrounded by family. She savors the fact she has at last, righted herself. Over time, the turmoil of her early years has vanished. What should she do for a finale? The garage walls are still overflowing with shelves filled with enormous quantities of leftover yarns. If she calculates properly, she can use it all up by the age of eighty. She considers, ten projects a year. That will do it. After all, she cannot leave those six healthy, towheaded grandchildren without warm hand-knits. She purchases two large dressers and hides them under a tarp at the back of the garage. After a year, one of the dressers is already filled with brightly colored caps, mittens, socks and sweaters.

What will the family think when they discover those dressers filled with hand knits after she is gone? She smiles and hopes they will think, *Gammie still loves us, even though she is no longer with us.*

Made in the USA
Charleston, SC
24 May 2011